The

Windwalkers

Of Xambic

By

STILLMAN WILSON

The Windwalkers Of Xambic

This book is a work of fiction. Any resemblance to people, places or events is purely co-incidental. Names, characters, events and places are either used fictitiously or are the product of the author's imagination.

ISBN: 978-0-9939335-3-0

Acknowledgement

Any and all of my works could not have been accomplished without the confidence of my wonderful loving partner and wife Irene.

To my talented daughter Amanda Wilson who takes the time from her novels to keep me on track with my writing.

ORBITING XAMBIC

"Rise and shine sweetheart."

"What the hell!" I said, sitting up, temporarily disoriented.

"We've put in nine hundred time clicks in the Andromeda sector. Nothing! Not a peep or a blip. Not a murmur."

"And your conclusion is?" I asked.

"My humble opinion is that the Federation has lost a lot of shipping in this sector and our mission is a failure."

"Wrong. If your crystals can't detect a magnadrive in this sector – the solution is pretty damn obvious."

"And that obvious solution is?" TC asked, her voice taking on just the faintest hint of amusement.

"Don't patronize me TC. If you can't see the answer when it's right in your face, don't get snide with me."

"The only conclusion I can draw is that you are due for a little R & R." TC said, her voice losing its lilt.

"I'm not deprecating you TC. Nobody could ever challenge that you employ the most powerful crystals in the galaxy."

"But?" TC said, bitterness creeping into her lovely voice.

"But nothing," I replied "I'm not one thousandth as intelligent as you and I don't have one billionth of your memory capabilities. However, I am a man and I see things man wise."

"Man-Wise! You pompous ass," TC cut in, anger in her voice.

"Yes Man-wise. I respect you for what you are. Why can't you respect me for what I am?"

The Windwalkers Of Xambic

"Oh I know you for what you are! You egotistical little fart!" she snorted.

TC and I had worked together as a deep-probe team for over four thousand years. And I still didn't understand her.

"All I've been trying to say is that your mind is so incredibly complex you have missed the obvious."

"Which is?" TC challenged.

"That if you can't find a trace of Federated activity, then it must stand to reason that none exists. That's my conclusion."

TC was silent for a minute. She was deep in examination of her crystals. "You're right, there is absolutely no activity."

"Then you forgive me?" I teased.

"You know I can't stay mad at you Marples," she purred, as only she could.

3

"If I'm forgiven, let's set sail for home."

Alpheratz was the brightest star in the Andromeda sector. And we were laying-to in her brightness.

"TC, how many rotations to light-warp plus 3?"

"Alpheratz will not bring us up to light-warp, never mind plus anything, commander." TC hummed, in her all-business mode.

"Fine. Give me the coordinates of a star that will. I want enough sling to take us to Sol with one jump."

"Circe has the mass, commander."

"How many clicks to Circe?" I asked, nervous about using the dreaded Circe as mass for a slingpass. "TC, are you sure Circe's the only black hole with enough mass to sling us home?"

The Windwalkers Of Xambic

"In this sector she is. But, we could hopsling using a black hole near Sirius." TC hummed.

"No - - The sooner the Federation is aware of the situation, the sooner a fleet of com-pac-probes can comb the Andromeda. Star by Star if necessary." I said.

"Any theories where the star cruiser and probes have gone?"

"Commander, I have ten thousand theories, but without a little hard evidence to support even one theory, they are worth spit."

"Spit?" I asked.

"You forget what spit is?" TC hummed.

"You trying to keep me on the straight and sane?" I asked.

"Do you need to be kept on the straight and sane?"

"You had better take the helm TC." I'm not comfortable setting up a slingpass around Circe, I thought.

"Nooo problems Tink. I'll swing-an -sway around that black devil until it screams, then we'll be zig-bang for home."

Ten clicks later we were in orbit around Circe.

Xambic gleamed blue as it orbited around Circe.

Xambic was the single waterbound planet that revolved around Circe. Circe a star with almost enough density to qualify it as a black star. Although Circe gave off a dull light in the blue-gold range, it had incredible mass not in proportion to its diminutive size. Only the Non Federated butchers of the Galaxy, the evil, bloodthirsty Singers, had really charted Circe.

In spite of the off-limits edict, we were now in our tenth rotation and soon would build enough slingpower to jump for Sol.

In mid-sentence, TC's lovely voice was suddenly static. Then she was gone, my ship shut down, and I dove for my emergency oxygen.

I had solved the mystery of Xambic. A spacecraft became an inert lump of useless junk when it entered the proximity of the appropriately named star - - Circe.

Xambic came into clear view. Somehow, I felt that with each revolution of this unknown planet, my dead ship was drawing nearer, to the least known about planet on Federated star charts.

My path of orbit had matched a band of white that circled an otherwise blue-gold planet, roughly the size of home planet earth. Never had I seen or even heard of a planet with a band around its equator. Never before had I heard of a planet with the power to change the path of a phomag drive.

The blue-gold surface that comprised almost the total surface of the planet was now completely distinguishable. It was liquid. I really hoped that it was water. The white band was now totally discernible as an unbroken band of what appeared to be sand.

I was not anxious, as a human, to set down on this weird planet. But as an explorer, it had questions I hoped I was going to solve without having to forfeit my life for that knowledge.

Old Drifter never wavered in course for even a second. Old Drifter was going to land on the white band, which was not close enough to view with my binoc. Soon, I would be splattered on the rocks that erupted everywhere. Or if I was lucky, just a skidding inferno from a sliding contact with the sand.

I estimated landing speed should be down to eight hundred miles a click. At ten miles from ground zero I opened the mechanical lock and hit the silk as Old Drifter faded into the distance. I had grave misgivings for my best friend - - locked aboard in her crystal -- without a chance of escaping.

All contact with the world as I knew it was gone from sight, and here I was floating ever so gently and slowly over the water. If it was water. I was an old hand at skydiving, and every other survival technique known to man. This was the deciding factor on the Federation choosing me from over four hundred larger Probe Commanders. Of all the geoprobe captains, I was the only Z-4 survivalist. And that fact had me in a position where these skills could save my life -- and hopefully they would!

As I drifted slowly out to sea I started to guide my chute into a path that would cross that of the closest island. I knew to miss it was certain death and to land on it would probably lead to the same fate. But right now, I was thankful for the incredible slow rate of descent, and the delicious unpolluted air. Never before had I actually tasted air!

In spite of my busy manipulations, I was heading for the drink. I drifted in like a fluttering moth. Somehow, I had the feeling that I could have almost kept from landing. Almost!

As I fluttered down, feather—light, to the surface, instead of hitting the release catch, I ran along the surface of the water, buoyed up by the parachute, certainly, but it was as if my determination was being felt by the living water below, and it was giving me the choice of entering, or walking along on it's surface. It was only a thought, and one that I had apparently not enough belief in for I settled in ever so lightly.

Buoyant, and relieved that the water was not acid or some other neat substance, I released my harness, then stripped to the raw. As I kicked off with my slow Aussie crawl, I knew I was swimming with greater speed and power than ever before.

The water felt cool and invigorating, and my skin felt radiant and alive. I tried a mouthful of water. It was delicious and sweet -- as I knew it would be. How could I know? Soon I was within clear sight of the beach. As I approached a small inlet in the island I stopped to tread water and rest for a moment. The current was not one that pushed me away from land, rather it was one that sensed my fatigue and was holding me up. If there was to be a current I knew somehow it would be one that washed me

ashore, and on a sandy beach, I
thought, laughing and taking in a
great mouthful of water. Laying on
my back, I squirted water through
the too-large space in my front
teeth. I am probably being lulled
into a false feeling of security
and some Circe-like monster is
probably singing to me a song of
contentment so that I'll drown,
and then it can eat my foolish
carcass, I thought to myself.
After all, the star was known as
Circe, and nothing was known about
this strange planet, other than
the fact that no spacer had ever
got off it. And I didn't want to
think about that. One problem at a
time, I told myself.

Even without expending energy I
could feel that I was being
carried towards a white beach and
I felt that if I bothered to swim,
I'd not arrive the sooner for my
troubles. A euphoria, bordering on
stupor, settled in, but I kept the
thought of the safe beach in mind,

and soon I was washed up on it. As I knew I would be. Somehow!

From my observations made while still aboard Old Drifter, I knew the island was twenty miles in circumference. Sitting on the incredible white sand at waterside, I cupped a handful of water to my mouth. It was not only not salty, it had an acidic tang—like weak lemon juice.

What a considerate planet, I mused happily, getting up and starting an examination of the island. But, without warning, a black wall of what could only be a typhoon, came over the horizon of this strange watery planet. This was my first contact with the dreaded typhoons that raced angrily and continuously over the face of this planet of mystery.

With the great black wall of water and shrieking wind rapidly approaching, I scuttled painfully across sharp stones, stones that

caused me difficulty in
penetrating the interior of the
small island, but I had no time to
sit and examine my feet for cuts.
I needed refuge from the rapidly
approaching typhoon. The howling
was rising in pitch. Soon I would
be part of it -- if I didn't find
cover. I wished for even a little
cave. And just as the howling
funnel approached, I found one. As
I limped on bleeding feet into a
depression barely large enough to
squeeze into, the howling wind
ravaged the island. Sheet
lightening filled the sky. High
overhead, I could see a group of
giant surfers riding the cottony,
white clouds that drifted along in
the wake of the typhoon. I knew
that I was experiencing a trauma-
induced hallucination—but rubbing
my eyes and pinching myself until
it hurt didn't rid me of the
vision on high. I could even hear
a mighty voice calling across the

The Windwalkers Of Xambic

swirling white clouds: "Stormrider – HO!"

Somehow I knew that this booming voice was directed at another giant. The other giant boomed back: "Windstriker – HO!"

From the safety of my cave, I enviously watched these two magnificent giants thunder across the sky. I drifted into sleep, only to waken to voices.

WATERMEN

"Big foon brought lotsa tasties,"
an impish voice said, and not far
from the cave.

And it spoke Galactic. I edged to
the lip of the cave.

"Look a ta foon brought ta us
Admural," rumbled a voice from a
great pink human.

"You speak Galactic!" I said.

"Everybody speakin Galactic – Big
deal," uttered a curly headed imp.

"Are you Federal Galactics?" I
asked hopefully.

"What's all o tha Galactic shit?"
asked a small human, hardly over
five foot. But, the human made up
for his small size by his
overbearing countenance. Great

green eyes and full lips pursed in a scowl, all the time huffing and puffing.

"How you be here?" asked the puffer.

"I fell out of the sky about four miles from this island."

"Right! An you be tripping aroun with ta Windwalkers," Guffawed another. This one was obviously good natured and amused by my predicament.

"Where be yer clothes, Grodatt?" the puffer demanded.

"Left them in the water, so I could swim," I answered.

"Shitty little Grodatt. First claims ta ride ta high winds nexta Windwalkers, now wants us ta believe he bin swimming in ta juice. Pretty good fer a Grodatt, course they talk it up good," came a rude reply from the black imp.

"What the hell is a Grodatt?" I said, rising to my full height of fifty-four inches. I strode out into the sun and stood with hands on hips and took a good look at my benefactors.

"Grodatt wants to know what's a Grodatt – Admural," the imp said, to the bulge-eyed leader of the motley crew.

"Ah Kenny, you knows Grodatts be goofy," replied the bug-eyed Admiral.

"He lookin ta be a Grodatt ta yuh Flubby?" asked Kenny.

"Bein fer surest," came a rumble from the huge being addressed as Flubby. He was easily seven feet tall, and quite possibly seven feet around the belly. He was very pink, and covered with freckles. His hair was red to the point of being almost orange. Flubby was huge for a Galactic.

The Windwalkers Of Xambic

"Lookin ta me he be a Mighty Windwalker," came a high pitched voice from a yellow skinned, sloe eyed male.

"Oh Meryl, sweeeet Giiirl!" Kenny laughed, mincing around the six foot thick-as-a-stick Meryl.

Flubby and Kenny laughed and danced in a circle around Meryl. The Admiral, only guffawed.

"Well if the game you morons are playing is, who can be the rudest, or the stupidest – My opinion is that you all come in first," I said.

They stopped laughing abruptly, each sensing something very wrong. I was to learn that a Grodatt never spoke in anger, and never had one ever left the Farthing of Longbottom.

"He sure be big fer Grodatt, Admural," Kenny said.

"Yar he be big ina snoot, an lookit his big hairy feet. He be

hairiest Grodatt ever I be seein,"
rumbled Flubby.

"You be one ta talk Flub. You be
as hairy as him," Kenny said,
laughing at Flubby, "and if he be
Grodatt cuz he be hairy. You be
giant Grodatt Flub." Kenny pointed
out.

"Why don't you just ask me who and
what I am?" I asked.

"Fair I say it. All bodies allus
jumpin ta stories about a person.
Hardly fair! I be sayin," Meryl
put in.

"No-bodies jumpin ta conclusions
bout you Mary!" Kenny giggled,
swishing around Meryl.

"Zactly what I mean!" howled
Meryl.

"Figurin ta start agin. I be
Admural MaQuig o ta Islanders
Imperial Navy, these my Royal
Marooners," MaQuig said.

"And I am Marples Tinkerman, captain of DeepProbe, Old Drifter of the Federated Galactic Commonwealth.

"That be ter same Federation a Singers comin from?" asked MaQuig, his eyes bulging.

"The Singers are here?" I asked.

"Friends of yourn?" insinuated MaQuig.

"Not likely! Nobody in the galaxy is dumb enough to even consider those horrors as part of anything. Other than a horrible death for the Federation itself."

"We only go by what we uns hearin, they claimin ta represent some kind a Federation. Claimin to be Bonas Fiders leaders o alla galaxies," Flubby growled.

"Bonas Fiders? How long have you been marooned on this planet?" I asked, deeply in fear of the answer.

"We haint marooned. We be proud ta say, we uns, an all who come before we uns bin on ta Islands longer o can be remembered," Flubby replied, looking to his comrades to see if they noticed how he was putting this offworlder in place.

"Have the Singers always been here too?" I asked, already knowing the answer, but curious to know if they knew anything.

"Nah, they be lousy offworlders. They trade fer stuff they be needin. They tradin mostly ta the Grodatts fer funny smoke," Flubby said, proud of his knowing more than me.

"Not really baccy likest we uns be smoking," corrected MaQuig.

"Yar, it be a kinda peep-weed. They callin it fwa-foo, only grows ta the Farthing of Longbottom," Kenny said, just starting to believe that I was not one of the wily little Grodatts, amusing itself at their expense.

"Yer really haint a Grodatt. Is yer?" he continued quietly, rubbing his great paws in discomfort.

"No. I am exactly who I say I am," I replied.

"Then I be beggin yer pardon fer havin bad manners an all. We bein rude cuz we thot you be a Grodatt." MaQuig sputtered, his face as red as the bare behind I couldn't hide.

"We haint no bully-boys ta strangers, specially them be needs help. Yer gotta admit yer be lookin as ta Grodatt, with yer dinky size and big nose an all," Flubby piped in.

"I can't begin to admit to anything, for I've never seen a Grodatt. If I could admit to having even the faintest idea what a Grodatt was like—I would be

23

guilty of misleading you fine gentlemen. I am guilty only of having my ship sucked down onto this planet." I said, my face almost as red as McQuig's.

"Double dare ta a Windwalker. He be talkin truth fer sure. He named us ta be gennlmen. A little one neverest name us ta be gennlemen. Not fer free fish by a load. By damn, we as caught us a Starman. What d'ya figure he be worth?" MaQuig asked his men.

I couldn't believe my ears. First – they apologized for not treating me right, because they were confused as to my identity. Now that they were sure – they quit insulting me, and obviously felt guilty about the insults, but not too guilty, for they were now deep in open conversation amongst themselves, as to what I was worth, and to who. "You louts are thinking of selling me?" I asked

in total disbelief at what I was
hearing.

"Nothin personal," Flubby said,
smiling.

"Nothing personal? Are you all
insane? You can't just go around
selling a human being," I
exploded.

"Why not?" MaQuig asked
suspiciously.

"Don't mean no harm-" Flubby
muttered, awkwardly.

"Because people can't go around
selling other people. It's bloody
well immoral." I said.

"Not be knowin bout what immoral
meanin, but pears to me, by what
yer claimin, yar not belong to
naughtbody. Seemin fair, if a body
findin that that naught belong ta
naughtbody --then, should be his
ta sell, or keep, as he who-found-
it likes," MaQuig huffed and
puffed, his great eyes all but
jumping off his face.

"Sweet Jesus —I'm captured by savages," I moaned.

"Savages!" they screamed indignantly in one voice.

"Yes savages, and real stupid ones I fear," I replied.

"We pologized bout havin poor manners, shows we haint savages, but you be soundin like one o them savages yourself. Bet you never glimmed a savage. You're closer a size a runty savage than we uns," Flubby rumbled.

"There are others?" I asked.

"Sure, plenty dumb Airheads, and Digabouts, and thieven Traders. Even be Shipwreckers. Only Grodatts and Twiggs be allus from here. Twiggs be savages, so they narent count, sometimes I be thinkin Grodatts be little better n Twiggs," Flubby said.

"What about the Singers? Do you consider them savages or civilized?" I asked MaQuig.

The Windwalkers Of Xambic

"Consider them foul monsters... That's what" MaQuig spat.

"Who do you civilized gentlemen plan on selling me to? Or are you planning on just peddling me around to the highest bidder?" I asked, sarcastically.

"I not be havin no profit," Meryl said, angrily.

"Nah. Not needs it." Flubby growled

"I seen from books -- how my people bin bought and sold. Don't think I be wantin nuthin Admural." Kenny muttered.

"So, that just leaves you and me MaQuig. And you might be a half a foot taller -- but without your men to overpower me, I think you had better re-evaluate your positon."

"Think yer scarin me, yer little runt?" MaQuig said, expanding himself to is full height of five foot.

"Don't expect to ever scare anyone. I've never met anyone my size," I grinned.

"What ta hell, this be in-sub-or-din-ation, maybe mutiny. You ever be hearin o mutiny?" McQuig leered, at his marooners.

"Listen MaQuig, I not be mindin you playin at ta Admural bullshit, but, if you be goin ter take it fer real ... yer can stuff it up yer nose!" Flubby said.

"Gonna be a fight. Bet a bale a baccy onta wooly little buggar," Kenny said producing a leather pouch out of his great coat.

"Wanna bet on yerself?" Kenny said, laughing at MaQuig.

"You can call me Tinkerman, not that other thing you just called me. If that's ok with you." I said smiling, but making my point. All the time keeping my eyes locked on the swollen orbs of MaQuig. Nobody offered to bet on MaQuig. This really set him off in a temper tantrum directed at everyone except me.

"Can whup yer, but being a Admural an all, have ta be thinkin bout portance o rank. Rollin in ta dirt wit a mere ... What be yer rank?" MaQuig expressed grandly, taking out a little leather bag and taking an over-dainty pinch of snooze. "Care for a pinch Captain Tinkerman?" only offering his snooze to me. Purposely ignoring his troops.

"Thank you I will Admiral," I said, as composed and dignified as I could, considering I was still naked.

"Perhaps as one gentleman to another ... I could prevail upon your courtesy as a fellow officer to loan me briches?"

"Certainly, we both bein officers an all," MaQuig said, now playing the role of fellow officer for all it was worth, and hoping his troops would forget about his reluctance to fight, without their help.

"Thanks," I said.

MaQuig and his Marooners were convinced that I must be related to the Grodatts, for everything about me shouted Grodatt at them, except the way I talked. As to my size: almost all of the shipwreckers were about six foot tall, including their women. Yet a few like Flubby were seven foot, and a few like MaQuig were barely over five foot: So size was not enough to judge me by. Nevertheless, they decided it was off to the Farthing for me.

Gentle winds moved the lateen rigged vessel through the water at a greater speed than I could believe. The ship was no more than bundles of bamboo tied together, with a sail of split bamboo woven into a fabric. "What be you thinkin o her?" MaQuig beamed.

The Windwalkers Of Xambic

"Sure is fast," I admitted.

"She be fastest, designed her myself," MaQuig said, aiming the bundle of driftwood into a small bay.

"She be not only fastest. She be onliest," Kenny said, to the amusement of the crew... And MaQuig glared.

A bay with a great, green toadstool of a mountain dominating the small bay. As we approached -- I could see that the toadstool of a mountain was more in the shape of a bent thumb.

THE FARTHING

We neared what looked like a bent-
green-thumb. A thumb that towered
at least a thousand feet over the
small adobe buildings huddled in
the tip of the tranquil harbor.
Small, brown, hairy people could
be seen coming down the face of
the gentle slope of the thumb.
They were all dressed identical to
my present garb, and that being
nothing more than a piece of
colorful fabric, from waist to
knee. Soon, the bundle of bamboo
was being pulled up on the white
sand by the morooners. I noticed
that not all the natives were
male, the females were the same
height as the males, but there the
similarity ended, while the black-
eyed males were covered from tip
of head to between the toes with
an abundance of short kinky hair,

32

the women were sleek of skin, and green of eye. The hairy, toad-like men were almost uniformly about four feet tall, with an occasional smaller one. One stood out from the crowd, as he was my size and had red hair.

"Greetings waterhe—men," the red-headed Grodatt grinned.

"Greeting constable mouser, where be yar major-minor? We be havin portant business ter conduct," MaQig replied affably, apparently not noticing the almost waterhead remark.

"Ican is down in da peep-patch, cutting a friendly. Soon he come him. Who dat?" the Mouser said pointing at me with his hoe.

"Was hopin you be tellin we uns." Flubby said, leaning over the small group in an attempt at friendly intimidation.

"Me never seen dat guy before," the mouser said, moving in to check out if I was taller than him. Deciding that I was no taller then himself, he smiled and hugged me. One by one, all the Grodatts approached me solemly, and each in turn hugged me with gusto. I noticed the females hugged me with even greater gusto than the males. Which was all right with me.

"What's your name?" a smooth-haired male asked, moving from the back toward the front of the Grodatts.

"I'm Marples Tinkerman." I said, showing my teeth in a nice even smile.

"Hmmmppp--- too much teeth," came a murmur from the crowd.

"Me Ican Grodatt. Me major-minor dis place, me very important in council of Greenleaf. You important trader?"

"No, I'm just an explorer."

"You don't have trade stuff?" Ican asked. Deciding that I had nothing to trade he turned to the other Grodatts. "Diss guy, just bum like waterheads."

Deciding I was of no importance, the crowd drifted away. I turned to ask MaQuig a question, just in time to catch the marooners pushing off the beach. Stranded on a backwards planet. Great! I went down to the wharf and sat with my feet in the water.

"Ho! Me Boozy Bentleaf, you like kakleberry?" a male Grodatt said, sitting down beside me.

"Ho yourself," I grinned, being careful not to show my teeth this time.

"You not Grodatt. Look like Grodatt," the Grodatt said, taking a swig from his leather wineskin. "Me give you good Grodatt name: You be Big Noleaf," Boozy grinned, showing very small flat teeth. I noticed that the Grodatt had absolutely no signs of canine teeth. Obviously his ancestors had always been herbivorous.

"Come ... Boozy show you garden. Good garden. Come." I was now in a state of near inebriation, and decided that anything was better than sitting with my feet in the water feeling sorry for myself. Walking up away from the beach towards the great bent thumb of green quartz, I noticed that on either side of the path there were small gardens. Each garden was surrounded by a one foot high wall of quartz. Stepping off the path into a garden about forty feet by sixty feet, Boozy declared proudly,"This my garden. Good fwa-foo."

"Fwa-foo?" I asked.

"Sure. Fwa-foo. You not know about peep-weed you?" Boozy asked, not believing anyone had not heard about the weed.

"I've never seen tobacco exactly like this," I admitted, feeling the sparkling leaf of a plant no taller than Boozy.

"This not baccy, this peep-weed, more better. You see," Boozy said, sitting on the small stonewall that was designed not to keep anyone out, but merely to serve as a boundary for each identical garden. These small gardens rose to the foot of the thumb, where the deep, black soil ended abruptly.

"Here try datt," Boozy said, handing me a small clay pipe, full of the soft leaf. Leaf that was covered with what looked to be diamond dust.

Boozy sat down and lit the pipe for me. No sooner had Boozy lit the pipe, when Mildleaf the Mouser, the total police force, and two other Grodatts appeared, as if from out of nowhere.

"Greetings my friends. Care to partake dat?" Boozy asked.

'Maybe justa puffle." the mouser
replied. "Forgot to introduce
properly at beach. Don't like
sneaky Waterheads. Don't trust any
of dem big peoples. Dey all steal
fwa-foo if I not watch careful.
Important job I got me. Me keep
all big devils from stealin peep-
weed. Anyhows I forgetting to
introduce proper. Proper name and
title much important to be first
timed by. You think so?" Mildleaf
grinned.

"I certainly do. Nothing is as
important as finding out exactly
what kind of people, people are."
I stated strongly, knowing somehow
that this was important to the
Grodatts.

"Good. Good. Good," came the happy
replies.

DILBO MINILEAF

Dilbo stepped forward shyly. "You not same as others," he stated simply. "They come to rob. Pretend to trade. You be friend to me?" The blue-eyed Grodatt asked quietly.

"I hope I can be a friend to all of you," I said smiling.

"I mean ssspecial friend." Dilbo stuttered, embarrassed.

"Yes. I can be your special friend." I said solemnly.   We hugged, as it was the custom of Grodatt.

"And dis is Riki Tiki, best trader in Grodatt. Also him best friend to Boozy Bentleaf. Dey got no wifes. Maybe dey be marry-mans to each an other."   Mildleaf said.

Riki Tiki and I hugged.

"Now I introduce to you proper. I be Mildleaf the Mouser, master warrior dat Farthing of Longbottom. Great Protector dat Greenleaf of peep. I be also capatan of police."

"You only police," Dilbo Minnileaf laughed.

"I still capatan," Mildleaf argued. "Anyway not to interrupt first formal greeting meeting. I also high officer of Council of Greenleaf," the Mouser continued triumphantly.

"All Grodatts high officers of Council." Dilbo said, his voice bubbling with mischief.

"Now you tell us proper who you are named," Mildleaf said. "My title is not so illustrious and as important as any here, but I am known formally as Marples Tinkerman, and I command a geoprobe starship for the Federation of Free Starmen."

They all bowed deeply to me in respect, then hugged, just to make sure the greeting was proper.

"First we give you smaller name. Good Grodatt name. Keep important proper name for dat formal telling only," Mildleaf said.

It took the comical, but serious little men, over a click to select a suitable name for me. They decided that because I had no plants, my last name should be Noleaf. And because during the discussion. I had informed them that a captain of a starprobe was merely a sort of jack-of-all-trades that just wandered around looking at things, and fixing what he could. This and that, I was a tinkerer, and that my name was Tinkerman ... Tink was a perfect name. Did I agree? When I did, they were overjoyed.

"I still like Big for best naming," Boozy complained, lighting a wooden match. I wondered where he had acquired the match, as it had been obvious from my repeated revolving of this planet that factories and technology were noneexistent.

I took a deep puff into my mouth, and held it as long as the Grodatts had. Then I exhaled. I was not a smoker, but wanted not to insult these sensitive little men. I liked the thought-- Sensitive LITTLE men. Always little had been a word used, almost behind my back, when referring to me. The smoke had a heavy, tangy aroma, and an oily pungency. I was just starting to consider the sweet smoke to be a form of very weak skunk weed, then it overpowered me.

Four clicks later I came to in a large bright room. The Grodatt with the incredible blue eyes was sitting at a small table looking out the one window. The room was of quartz, with great thick veins of gold, and pale green quartz breaking up the white. The soft pattern was relaxing to the eyes. "How are you feeling?" Dilbo Minnileaf asked, not turning. "How did you know I was awake?" I asked. Still having not moved a muscle other than my eyelids.

"You will learn my friend. Yes I see that you have much to learn, and then you can teach me. And I in turn will teach my simple brothern," Dilbo said quietly.

"What happ--" I started to ask.

"First we eat. Then I will endeavor to answer your many questions. Do you eat meat? Or are you a vegetarian. I see by those terrible canines you possess that your ancestors were indeed animal killing savages."

"What happened to your quaint ignorance?" I challenged.

"Ah ... I see that you are aware of your environment already. That is good. It shows strength to recover so quickly. Some have taken months, and were never the same. Most are as you see them. The weed has taken away the murderous instincts from the large off-worlders that are marooned but it apparently does little for their gray matter. Only the Singers remain intelligently evil."

An incredibly diminutive woman came from another room and put an enormous gold plate of food on the one table.

"Come. Eat. It will fortify you," Dilbo Minnileaf said.

The small woman returned from what was apparently a cooking room. This time she was carrying a splendid jug of hammered gold.

"You are shocked by our use of gelt I see."

"Yes, for in our galaxy it is extremely rare, and considered precious." I said.

"Here it is our only metal. We have no other. Does that explain anything?" Dilbo asked, selecting a thick slice of melon, and eating it daintily with his fingers. "Come eat. It is better to talk on a full belly."

I stood on legs, not unstable, but with an incredible feeling of lightness. A lightness that gave me the same odd feeling that I had experienced while running over the water, still in my chute.   I really felt that if I just knew how-- I could spring off the porch and walk for clicks-- In the air.

"Before we eat. I had better introduce you to my venerable mother. Mother, this is Tink Noleaf. And this is my mother, Winiferd Minniplant." Dilbo said proudly, reaching down and putting his arm around his tiny mother. In spite of her advanced years. Winiferd blushed. I could see that she was not coming forward for the customary hug, so I did. Winiferd turned from pink to bright red. Dilbo and I laughed. Winiferd fled to the kitchen.

"You've made a conquest. Mom took to you. Mom has the best sight on Flightless. I knew I was right about you."

"And that is?" I asked.

"Too soon to tell you who you are. Soon come."

"Soon come?" I asked, stepping out onto the porch with a glass of the amber drink. "What is this unbelievable drink?"

"Unfermented Kakleberry." Dilbo replied.

About two miles from the almost-cliff dwelling, could be seen what appeared to be a black pond, with a glistening island in its center. I turned to ask what it was.

46

The Windwalkers Of Xambic

"You have spotted the dirt in the pudding." Dilbo said. I looked again to the pond.

"What is it?"

"That pond represents the troubles that are brewing on this otherwise very peaceful planet. The fwa-foo has kept us safe from all other shipwreckers, but it has become our undoing in the hands of the Singers."

"Are they the Andromeda Singers?" I asked.

"The same."

"Then your planet has a serious problem. These evil creatures are a blight wherever they are. They have always had strange power, and any planet they manage to infiltrate, they soon take over shipping and trading. With their Tetrahedron-web they can mind-move anything on the face of any planet. Recently it has been reported that they have figured a way of moving matter from planet to planet. Possibly even from galaxy to galaxy." I said. Unable to keep the concern from my voice.

"Then your trip here is as I suspected."

"And that is?" I asked.

"I think your geoprobing is what you do, but I think that you came specifically to spy on the Singers. And Xambic brings all down who get too close. Even the Singers came that way. Some say that the Twiggs and Grodatts share a common ancestry and it is from another galaxy ... Some say ..."

"And you. What do you say?" I asked.

"I say, I have the proof of all beginnings. Even to the history of the allusive Windwalkers."

"The Windwalkers are real?" I asked.

"Yes. They exist but they are seldom seen up close."

"They sure appeared to be huge. Big enough to have trouble hiding," I said remembering the apparitions in the sky.

"You saw more than one! Mother! Tink actually saw more than one Windwalker."

"I knew that before the waterheads brought him. The problem is that the Singers know of his existence. Right now they don't know of his whereabouts but when they do, they will be sending their Grunts in droves to get him. We must prepare my son, for this one could free us."

"Mother! You stopped the waterheads from delivering Tink to the Singers... Didn't you? You actually put a control on them from over thirty miles."

"Over ninety miles," the miniature lady said shyly."

"Ninety miles!" Dilbo exclaimed in awe.

"Yes and the Singers were singing ever so pretty to those waterheads. By now both Singers and Watermen will be furious, but they will not find you young man, for I see that your will is strong and Mother Nature looks kindly upon you, for who else caused your landing near the Island."

"But you stopped those nitwits from selling me?"

"I did tamper ever so lightly. She did most of it."

"Can you read minds?" I asked.

"Minds I can peek into and sometimes persuade but the control over wild physical substance is more than my mild talent can accomplish. Only nature can control nature, even the Windwalkers can only ask, but they do it with gusto. And sometimes

Mother Nature listens," Winifred Minniplant said, smiling kindly.

"My god! I'm on a planet of magic." Hope creeping into my mind for the first time.

"No. No magic exists my friend. Come into my library and you can read for awhile. It may help." Dilbo said leading me into a small room. Pressing a hidden switch caused a small dresser to swing away from where it had previously appeared to be built into the wall. A tiny staircase had been carved into the rock.

It was an extremely tight fit for me and I could see that it would be impossible for any of the offworlders. Dilbo had a very private library indeed. After climbing vertically for over three hundred feet we reached a huge room. Soft light was coming in through the solid glass-like wall. "What do you think?" Dilbo asked sitting on a low chair.

"Tell you when I get my breath." I gasped, flopping into another chair.

"The Twiggs lived here. It was far in the past and Twiggs were not thought well of then. My forefathers didn't understand the little savages, and ran them off. Mom and Dad were the first and only ones to share cultures.

"That is why your mother is so small. She isn't a Grodatt."

"No. Mom is a Twigg, and even I am often confused by her but Dad loved her with great heart and Mom still loves him."

"Then your father is not dead?"

"Not as long as Mom thinks otherwise. He was taken by the Singers over ten years ago. Only Mom has hope."

"If you get your ability to peek from your mother. Does that mean the rest of the village is just as mind -blind as me?" I asked, looking around the auditorium sized room of wall-to -wall books. "Does anyone else know of your talent?"

"No. They all suspect Mom of course but it ends there."

Most of them actually think of Mom as being a Grodatt. For she is a full foot taller than most Twiggs. Then again, she is a foot shorter than the average four foot Grodatt."

 "Are there still tribes of Twiggs?" I asked.

"No, they are now only family units. And they don't come out of the deep sands any longer. Some say they live in the tunnels of the Sandshrieks.

"Sandshrieks?" I asked.

"Yes Sandshrieks. You really don't have any information about Xambic do you?" Dilbo said, scanning me till I felt a sudden surge of nausea, the same nausea that I had experienced when Winnie had scanned me.

"No, we know almost nothing about Xambic. All our instruments for observation have no ability to penetrate the atmosphere of this weird planet. And any that land have never been heard from again. That is why I'm here." I said.

"Then you are a spy for the Federation?" Dilbo said.

"No. Not a spy. Rather a tinkering observer."

"But your mission is to report what is happening. Isn't it?" Dilbo said, grinning, knowing he had me in a position where my answer would be an admission about my mission.

Dilbo scanned me ever so lightly.

"Quit that will you." I demanded. Just a little angry at the invasion of my privacy.

"You can tell when I scan you?" Dilbo asked.

"Not only can I tell but it makes me dizzy and the stronger you probe the worse it gets."

"That's wonderful!" Dilbo exclaimed excitedly.

"What's wonderful about almost passing out? Feeling like I'm going to vomit all over myself is hardly exciting."

"Don't you see what an advantage it can be?" Dilbo asked, holding both of my hands and gazing deep into my face.

"NO. I don't," I replied, with just a touch of anger in my voice, as I broke the eye-lock and pushed Dilbo away with slight force.

"Oho. You don't understand," Dilbo exclaimed. "You can never have a Singer or anyone sneak up and scan you. You immediately become sick. And I've noticed that the stronger the scan the sicker you become. I have a feeling a deep-probing total-reap-scan of a Singer would cause you to pass out."

"And this is an asset?" I asked.

"Certainly it's an asset. For the Singers are sight blind, and rely on the scanning to track their prey. They have the ability to broadcast an over-blanket of probe over an area. That's how the Grunts capture us. They come in fast under the over-blanket and we are unable to protect ourselves, as we are unaware of them. But with you in a war party we could never be approached without knowing it. They could no longer sneak up on us! Just think of it." Dilbo exclaimed his face shining with excitement.

"Sounds like a lot of fun for me." I said wryly.

"Don't think of the negative aspects. Try and see what a positive factor this can be against the Singers.   And I know you have been sent to spy on the Singers."

"How do you know?" I challenged.

"Well if you were here under the goodwill and friendship of the Singers, you would have come in through a tetrahedron-web, but you didn't. You shipwrecked. And now they are looking for you with malevolent sincerity. Doesn't take a certified genius to figure out what's happening."

"Maybe I'm here to spy on you Grodatts," I laughed.

"Sure. We're such a big threat to the Federation. I doubt that the Federation knows that any life exists on Xambic other than the Singers. What do you say to that Mister Explorer?"

"I say you're smarter than you look and that there is a greater problem here on Xambic than the Federation has even the smallest clue of. Somehow the Federation must be warned."

"Finally we are in agreement. What do we do?"

"I know exactly what must be done. The Federation must be apprised of the situation here on Xambic. These damn Singers have this whole planet in quarantine. Actually they have it in thrall. Subjugation and enslavement by any species over any other species within the Federation is criminal. The Singers have the ability to open this planet up to the freedom of the Federation by making their Tetrahedrons available to all."

"But they are not physically holding us prisoner."

"Actually they are, Dilbo. For to withhold help is as criminal in some instances as actually committing an active offense. Suppose you came upon a helpless child in the wilds. A child that was starving to death and you just left it to die, when you had the means to save it. While you had not set out to commit an active crime your failing to help is itself a crime."

"What if you passed a child in a city that was starving to death?" Dilbo asked coyly.

"And do you have knowledge of its starving?" I asked, looking hard at Dilbo.

"I'm only presenting a hypothetical situation," Dilbo defended. "I could never let a child starve."

"Nor should anyone. But the crime is in the knowledge. For without the knowledge that the child was starving there is no purposeful intention of letting it starve."

"Then it is the intent that is the crime? Not the actual act?" Dilbo said watching me closely, but not attempting to scan even a little.

"True. Without conscious intent it is an unfortunate incident but nothing more." I said smiling.

"That may be true for a crime of inactive response. But what of an active crime where one kills another? How then could you say it was other than a crime? For to take a life is to take a life. Fancy thoughts and words do not change the fact that a life is taken. Intent or none-intent will certainly not bring a life back." Dilbo argued.

"No. it will not change the fact that a life has been taken, but it is only the intention to do so that is the crime. The actual act is not a crime."

"How so?" Dilbo challenged.

"Supposing you were cutting a tree for firewood and it fell on someone killing them. Are you guilty of a crime?"

"Not if I took precautions," Dilbo replied.

"But if in spite of your precautions the tree did fall and kill someone. Is it a crime?" I asked.

"No. For it would be an accident."

"Right! But what if you knew that someone followed a path every day that put them in line for the tree to fall on them and you timed it so that the tree fell on them doing an injury. Is this a crime?" I continued.

"Certainly," Dilbo replied.

"Now. What if you tried to do injury but missed with the tree. Is this a crime?" I asked.

"Not on Xambic. Is this a crime in your Federation?"

"Yes. While the outcome is not so severe the intent is no different than if the act was consummated as planned. In the Federation to conspire to a crime shows total intent to commit the crime, therefore, we view it with great severity in our courts. The only difference is that the act of conspiracy is hard to prove."

"What if a member of your Federation thinks about committing a crime?" Dilbo pressed on with his argument.

"Unless they actually planned it, and it could be proved they had intentions of carrying out the plan. Nothing."

"What if a member of your Federation threatened to do grave bodily harm to another person yet never carried it out?"

"That would depend but in the eyes of our courts the threat implies cold blooded intentions, while on the other hand two members of our Federation could become angered with each other and a terrible beating or even death could be the outcome. While the act is no different the intentions can't be proven beyond a reasonable doubt therefore it is not considered to be as terrible a crime," I plodded on tired of the conversation.

"I don't understand your justice system." Dilbo replied.

"Most of us don't either but we believe it is the fairest to the greatest number of our citizens."

"But if you don't like it why not change it?"

"We change it constantly," I responded.

"Am I making you angry with me?" Dilbo asked.

"You're not thrilling me."

"You have been honest with me. You have put up with my berating you about a subject that you yourself can do nothing about yet you have been honest, and no emanations of anger have clouded your mind. I will not test you again."

"This has been a test?" I asked.

"Yes it was required, and if it's any consolation. I haven't enjoyed it either." Dilbo said discomfort showing on his face.

"Yes I suppose that you have to be sure that I'm not an agent for the Singers. Are you sure now?"

"Better than me being sure. Mom is sure."

Out of the desert came a small party of warriors on foot. Each armored Grunt carried a weapon that I could see even from the refuge high in the hill. The weapon was a tube that fired a projectile by means of an explosive charge.I had trained with similar devices taken from the Archives of Ancient Armament.

Hundreds of warriors armed with such devices would not stand against a single geoprober equipped with standard Federation anti-personnel equipment. However, I had nothing except my training. And that would have to do if I was going to break the stranglehold the Singers had on Xambic. And if not stopped soon, a stranglehold they would have on the Federation of Free Starmen as well.

"These are not true Singer-warriors Dilbo," I said moving away from the window-wall of quartz.

"We are quite safe here as these Grunts have no psi ability but they know you're here. I can feel their eager anticipation of being rewarded for delivering you to their masters. It frightens me to be near these stupid creatures," Dilbo told me, a frown of concern puckering his young face.

"Can they get in here?" I asked.

"No, but you can't leave either. We have never needed an escape exit. Only the Twiggs can work the geltstone."

"We need an exit now," I said.

"Must be at least twenty Grunts," Dilbo said grinning.

"Hardly seems a reason for joy." I said gloomily.

"They'll be out of the garden path in a few seconds and camped right at our door." Dilbo said.

"How long will that take? I have had dealings with Grunts on other planets and I can tell you they will park in front of your door until the sands of time turn to stone."

"That may be but the sand front of our house will never turn to stone. In fact it should be jumping with life anytime."

Below in the white sands the Grunts began setting up a camp. They knew that the small round doorway was too small to permit even a small Grunt entering. They had enough explosives to blow the door but the Singers had ordered them not to waste the explosives on the strange stone that the thumb-shaped mountain was composed of. Real Singer-Warriors had tried in the past. And the Singers were not looking to repeat that fiasco.

All knew that Mhyn Mountain was unbroachable.

Twiggs had formed all the housey and garden chambers far in the past then suddenly they had left this indoor mountain city and disappeared into the shifting sand. Some said they lived in outcroppings of geltstone. Others said they lived with the young Sandshrieks. Occasionally a lone Twigg would appear to trade for milkathing cheese. They would trade highly prized and valuable jewelstones for a little cheese.

The honest Grodatts tried to refuse the jewelstones and just give the small strange Twiggs the coveted cheese but this would

bring sadness to the otherwise
perpetually amused faces of the
Twiggs. Not wanting to offend nor
drive the strange little people
away the Grodatts took the
jewelstones, but promptly brought
them to Iffy Grodatt for storage.
Iffy would squirrel them away. And
even her marry-man to be Dilbo
Minnileaf, dared not enter her
squirrel room. Someday, the Twiggs
could need their jewels. And Iffy
had them stored. Every last one of
them.

The Singers knew of this, and had
hatched several attempts at
broaching the housey of Iffy but
the great thumb of geltstone
permitted no intrusions.

The single round portal that
opened into a common tunnel which
all the houseys of the Grodatts
shared was said to be a living
portal. And it only let those
enter that had no harmful
intentions.

68

The Windwalkers Of Xambic

It was further believed that the great thumb-shaped fortress of geltstone was a living stone that protected those that it chose to live with in symbiosis. But these were only rumors.

In front of the portal, the Grunts formed a semicircle and busied themselves with setting up camp.

"It looks as if they plan on a protracted siege. The Singers must really want you badly to commit such a large well-armed force." Dilbo said smiling, and obviously not impressed with the Grunts parked right on his doorstep.

"I don't know what you're so all-fire amused about Dilbo, you're just as much a prisoner as I am, and how will the rest of the village get in or out with those Grunts practically parked in the doorway?" I said my annoyance showing.

"Do I detect anger maybe even distrust?" Dilbo said.

"I don't distrust you but yes I am
a little ticked off with having
those morons out there. You may
not be aware of their tenacity but
I am and they are anything but
funny. They've been ordered to
guard the portal, and they'll do
so until they starve to death or
are given a countercomand. What is
amusing about this?" I said,
hotly.

"Look! The village has come for
the fireworks," Dilbo said.

"Fireworks?" I asked looking in
all directions for anything that
could mean fireworks.

"Have you not noticed that these
grunts are carrying metal
firetubes and other metal
objects?" Dilbo asked.

"So what." I replied.

"These Grunts have just come
through the time-web of the
Singers and are even now on the
living sand for the first time.

70

The Windwalkers Of Xambic

Actually I am surprised that it is taking so long for the shrieks to make an appearance.

"Shrieks?" I asked.

"Sandshrieks to be exact. Nowhere on Xambic is there a gram of metal other than gelt. Better than an explanation is a living demonstration. And I sense the young shrieks are very close. Watch the camp carefully for you are shortly to view a sight that you will never likely see again."

Below in a full circle every man, woman and child of Grodatt were sitting on the stone garden walls, children held high. To better see whatever was about to obviously take place. Obvious to everyone but me and the armed Grunts who were now forming a line facing what they believed to be a threat by the villagers.

The villagers responded to the Grunts armed stance with hooting and laughter.

"Has the village never faced armed Grunts before?"

"Not armed." Dilbo replied not taking his eyes from the scene below. Even the taciturn Winnie Minniplant could not take her eyes from the Grunts below.

Out of the deep of the endless desert came a rippling of the sand. Overhead storm clouds were forming in an otherwise cloudless sky. A bolt of lightning struck the ground a few hundred feet from the Grunts. And where it had, the sand boiled. It boiled with what appeared to be hundreds of high tension wires thrashing against each other. Shooting and arcing in a profusion of short yellow and longer blue flashes.

Quickly, the shrieks formed a living wriggling, blanket of electricity. Electricity that filled the clearing. Screams of terror could be heard from the Grunts who were now completely

72

engulfed by the shrieks. As suddenly as they came, the shrieks were gone and with them all metals and other foreign elements not of a living nature. Not a Grunt had been hurt in even the smallest way.

"Not very formidable without weapons and body armor are they?" Dilbo giggled.

The Grunts were confused and disoriented without their fine black body armor to hide behind. Twenty warriors who slept since boyhood with sword and gun were now facing what they considered to be an armed and hostile village. And to make the situation even more embarrassing a wild comalong was moving around them curiously with its long trunk sniffing them.

They all knew of the poisonous beak that lay hidden in the end of its long trunk, and with not even a stick to defend their very private parts, they fled to the

safety of the six tetrahedrons
and the milky web that they had
just arrived through.

The village roared in laughter.

WILD PIGGOTY INN

"While they are busy getting bamboo body armor and ironwood bo-staves we had better get you into the village."

"Is the village safe?" I asked.

"For the time being it will be, as the Singers can't get a reading as long as you stay in very close proximity to at least ten mind shields. Independently they can penetrate our shields, but if we stay in groups of ten they have no control over us nor can they get even a small reading. We never travel in groups of less than ten for that reason. They don't even try to read the village as it gives them severe headaches for days after."

Almost on the heels of the retreating Grunts. I followed

Dilbo across the now empty sandy lawn that separated the fortress from the jade gardens of fwa-foo.

"This is indeed a strange place!" I exclaimed.

"Moreso than you will ever know." Dilbo replied.

"Moreso than you know?" I asked grinning.

"Moreso than anyone will ever know." Dilbo laughed.

We approached the comalong. It sniffed up to me and snorted twice. Its great ears suddenly sticking out like two blue woolly radar antennas. I tried to walk around it. The woolly creature moved quickly in my way and snorted again.

"She likes you!" Dilbo exclaimed.

"Is that good?" I asked nervous about the beak.

"If a comalong snorts at you, you have made a friend for life.

The Windwalkers Of Xambic

Bigstick is the only other none-Twigg that a comalong has ever snorted at. You have just been paid a rare compliment."

"I'd probably appreciate the compliment a lot more if I didn't know about that beak," I said.

"They use the beak to render Sandvipers harmless."

"What do they do with them then?" I asked.

"Sandvipers are the main food of both Twiggs and comalongs. I gather your planet has no Sandvipers."

"Actually we have all kinds of poisonous snakes. It's just that we have nothing like your comalongs. We do have an animal that resembles a comalong only it eats hay. But at a distance a baby African elephant could be mistaken for a comalong. That is it is about the same size and shape but it's not covered in blue wool and

it squirts water and feeds itself
with it's trunk. It doesn't go
around poisoning things."

"The comalong feeds itself with
its trunk. And it certainly
doesn't go around poisoning
anything. It just eats Sandvipers.
And we here on Xambic don't mind
that a bit," Dilbo defended. The
Comalong snorted twice and nudged
me.

"She's right. We had better head
for the village before those
darned Singers re-arm the Grunts."

I followed Dilbo, and the woolly
comalong followed close behind,
grunting happily to herself as she
paddled along on great flat feet,
her long nose swinging from side
to side. I noticed as we entered
the village that its streets were
of the same sparkling sand as the
roadway.

"How come the road in the village
is not bricked or at least hard
packed?" I asked.

The Windwalkers Of Xambic

"The living-sand is our friend. It's the home of the Sandshrieks. Without the sand we would be vulnerable to attacks by off world weapons."

"What about moving heavy objects?" I asked.

"We don't move anything heavy. We never have and we don't see any reason to start. I have read that on your planet you are burdened with so many possessions as to totally lose your own identity. You are even judged by all the material objects that you clutter your lives with. We don't need to be reassured by piles of material objects," Dilbo said. "We don't need material objects to reassure us who we are. I've read that on your planet that even your clothing is a symbol of who and what your social status is."

"Unfortunately by some." I replied thinking about it.

"We have different values here. You may see us as primitive but hold off making a judgment on us." Dilbo said.

"I will if you will." I said.

The Wild Piggoty Inn was the hub of the Farthing. It was a simple blue clay and straw building with a deeply thatched roof of silver rush. It was larger than any building in the Farthing of Longbottom and was a combination rooming house for visitors and meeting place for open meetings of the Council of Greenleaf.

The ground level floor was made of heavy planks laid on the white sand. White sand could be seen between each smooth plank. Heavy wooden tables and benches filled the room. A monstrous fireplace dominated one wall. In it four huge birds roasted over bright coals. And as I was soon to learn, the Wild Piggoty Inn was the only eating establishment in the Farthing to serve meat.

It was also the only pub, rooming house and meeting hall for the public. The second floor was just a simple pair of open lofts that were open down the middle. One side was used for storage of food stuff and was the living quarters of Mumma Broadleaf and her marryman, Ican Grodatt the Major minor of the Council of Greenleaf.

They had their secure-housey in the fortress of Mhyn as did all the Grodatts. But like the other Grodatts other than Dilbo and his mother, they lived in the adobe village. Only Dilbo and Winnie Minniplant lived in the fortress full time. Only in times of peril for the village did the rest of the council seek refuge in the fortress.

The other half of the loft was reached by a ladder and that whole side was ranged with sleeping pads

packed with fresh, sweet, sea-
grass, gathered by the traders
from Rockapile.

"Greetings Mumma. I have brought
a friend to stay awhile."

"Any friend to you be welcome at
dat Wild Piggoty," Mumma Broadleaf
said smiling showing small flat
even teeth.

How'll I pay for my keep?" I asked
Dilbo.

"Nobody pays in actual cash. We
are without commerce as you know
it. You just sort of do what you
can to contribute to what is going
on around you." Dilbo said.

"That can't possibly work," I
said.

"It does with us who live in the
village. With off-worlders we sit
in the courtyard behind the Inn at
high noon on a time we have
anything to trade. Others who wish
to trade do the same. Trading
without the sunlight and our

fellow Xambicers to view in the open is forbidden to Grodatts." Dilbo said quietly.

"How do you control others from breaking your laws?"

"Not laws. Just the way we do it Tink."

"Then you don't make others obey this rule?"

"No. But if they cheat and lose face in the dark then honest traders won't sit in the courtyard with the offenders."

"And that works?"

"Works just fine. You'll see."

"Yes.I suppose I'll be here for awhile."

"You'll be here forever." Dilbo said, his great blue eyes reflecting his sadness for me.

"And that forever will be short if the Singers get their way. But I was to get information for the

Federation. I have never failed on a mission. This one will just take all my ability to assimilate enough information to solve this chess game. Once I have all the information that is here then I'll find a way to send it on to the Federation."

"That still won't help you get off Xambic."

"No. But it will save countless lives, if I can stop these terrible Singers," I said, noticing that Dilbo was becoming highly excited by the appearance of a small party. They had just entered, and were seating themselves by the fireplace.

"Who are they? They must be pretty terrible to have you so upset."

"You can tell I'm upset?" Dilbo asked, looking at me strangely.

"Quit it!" I told him, as I could feel a touch of nausea.

The Windwalkers Of Xambic

"It isn't me. It must be Nhioby. She's very powerful. But she knows better. The Piggoty is neutral grounds. We'll straighten this out right now," Dilbo said, taking my hand and marching me over to the table of newcomers.

"Who is responsible for the probe?" Dilbo asked, angrily. The two boys just looked to one another and giggled. They both wore heavy gray pigotskin jumpsuits, with enormous pockets everywhere. Their skin was almost as grimy as their soiled clothing. Each young boy had four braided take-my-head handles of greased hair.

The man seemed discomforted by the giggling of the boys. He looked away from the scene to the fire. His stark white hair hung to his waist in wild disarray but it was very clean as was the almost transparent skin of his long, large hands that peeped out from under his black tunic of a fur unknown to me.

His face was almost entirely hidden by his hooded greatcoat of the same rare luxurious black fur. He turned his gaze in my direction, and the two blackest eyes I had ever been scrutinized by took in my whole being with a glance. I knew the glance, as I had faced it before only never so completely. Satisfied as to who and what I was he turned his arrogantly handsome face to the boys at his table.

"Be minding your manners when you're in the presence of your betters." he uttered in a whisper. "You'll excuse my sons and my beautiful Nhioby too I fear. For that is why you have come to our table is it not? My good and noble councilor?" he said in a totally controlled and whisper-like voice.

The Windwalkers Of Xambic

Looking at me now was an amused, but I could also detect, just slightly embarrassed man.

His black eyes, and strong nose, were all that could be seen of for a face as the rest of it was hidden by his immense coal-black beard. A beard that was so unlike that of his hair, in that it was well brushed and braided here and there as if done by a playful child while the father slept. His great black beard was glistening whether from the pomade or just good grooming I could not tell. But both this strange man who could look deep into a being without ESP, and his wild but beautiful consort appeared to have less than nothing in common with the grinning louts they sat with.

But he had named them sons. The last member of the party was attired in a one piece gauze jumpsuit that exposed more than it concealed. She too had a hooded greatcoat made of the same glistening, black fur, as her companion. Her Violet eyes dominated a face of the whitest cameo-like beauty that I had ever seen. If there was a resurrection of Helen of Troy, surely it was this strangely exotic woman.

She threw her hood back and shook out a black cloud of hair that reached her ankles. Knowing that she was tantalizing me she stood and removed her greatcoat. I was physically stunned by her

With a sensual, yet cold laugh, Nhioby tossed her head and her hair enveloped her as completely as the great coat had. She returned to her chair, sitting with her legs tucked under her. Satisfied that all eyes in the Piggoty were on he she laughed, showing small white pointed teeth. Not unlike those of a very amused cat.

"Enough Nhioby," came the whisper, softly, then with a slight tinge of harshness. "Leave the table. If you will." he grinned at his sons showing a greater quantity of strong white teeth than I could believe it possible to cram into one mouth.

"I must apologize for both my sons and my mate. They are equally rude in their different ways. But I am a poor man that can do nothing to change them," he said, smiling that predators mouth full-of-teeth smile, that somehow conveyed anything but warmth.

"Be seated gentlemen. If you please," came the whisper.

I could feel both amusement, and intelligence, in that soft energy-saving voice. And I could detect madness just under the surface. I knew that madness was most probably the order of every day for this foursome. A slight nausea flushed me and was instantly gone.

I looked up to see the beauty he had called Nhioby smile as a child will when caught, and knows it is not going to be punished.

"This lovely creature is the light of my life. She is my Nhioby. I understand that I am referred to as Kookerman, although this isn't my name, I will answer to it without bearing you malice. These two wonderful sons by a-finding are Bulbus and Breezy. It probably matters not that you call them by the right names. As I am sure they are unaware of even their names. But enough of us. Who can you be?"

"Dis is my good friend Tink NoLeaf," Dilbo put in quickly.

"No one is listening Dilbo," Kookerman said with a full voice, that was actually quieter than his whisper.

"Whaaa—" Dilbo started to challenge.

"Never mind, good and noble Grodatt. If you wish to continue with your public masquerade in private. This is your business. I only supposed that you would be more comfortable conversing freely without all those foolish dees and dose, and dems and dats, but it is entirely up to you," Kookerman purred then punctuated his statement by holding both hands palms up, opening his electric black eyes, till they were large and round, his smile turning his mouth into a den of teeth.

We three men laughed.Nhioby looked on in scorn.

"If you are not the illiterate you seem, and if your friend is not another very large Grodatt, and if I know this already, you must ask yourself if the Singers know of your well-kept, deep unsecret? If they do not know, then you malign me in your unsaid thoughts. And if they do, am I the hidden agent? Or do they even have one? I have heard it whispered about, that I am so without direction that you, Dilbo Minnileaf would not trust me to take a trade order for a single fish and expect me to do that simple transaction correctly... because I am so addled."

"This is no-" Dilbo started to argue.

"Come now. You are known as an honorable councilor. Why do yourself this dishonor of saying that which we both know to be an untruth." Kookerman purred showing an array of white.

"What of Nhioby?" Dilbo asked quietly.

"What of Nhioby?" Kookerman chuckled. "Nhioby above all, is not interested in the petty happenings on this forlorn sandball. She was the Reigning Queen of Nhark answerable to no one, and as her proud ancestors before her, less interested in their petty squabbling and childish political positioning. Do you think she could show anything but disdain for these foul spiders?"

"Nhioby is the missing Queen of Nhark?" I asked in shock.

"Yes!" Kookerman hissed.

"My god! Then you are the missing Crown Prince Nyzerabad, High Lord of all the Nyzan Common Free Federated Dynasty. Even now our Federation is working for a unified agreement with your Federation." I said in awe and shock. I could not believe my ears, but looking at the incredible Nhioby with this disturbing information as a guide. I could see that this mad-looking but quiet man, spoke the truth.

"Then how do you account for your sons?" Challenged Dilbo.

"An astute observation for a
supposed illiterate clod.
What say you? Master Minnileaf?"
Kookerman said, grinning.

Dilbo just sat silently as one
whapped with a rubber mallet.

"My god! And we all believe you to
be nothing more than a mad group
of..."

"Thieven imbeciles," Nhioby said,
without malice.

"Ahhhhhh but..." Dilbo tried to
speak.

"My sons are of course not our
children. We shipwrecked on this
terrible planet four years ago.
The Island we wrecked on was
populated by twin ten year old
boys. Boys who had neither speech,
nor knowledge of anything other
than surviving. When we crashed on
the island that they were on, they
daily gathered food for Nhioby and
Nhioby can't bear to send them
away. Even if they are offensive.

94

The Windwalkers Of Xambic

She argues that if I could rule the most volatile society in the Galaxies in peace and harmony, why could I not help these poor unfortunates?"

"Nhioby thinks like that?" Dilbo asked confused.

"Occasionally," Kookerman smiled for the first time without it being a threatening gesture. "Occasionally my beautiful Queen is very very kind. Is that not so my love?" Kookerman purred, taking both her milk-white hands in his almost transparent one.

At a closer inspection I noticed that they both had small pointed ears hidden by their incredible abundance of hair. And I could see the large delicate hands of Kookerman had retractable claws. Yes, I knew his story was true, I was in the presence of the most singly powerful entity in two Federations. And I knew that his great power was arrived at in his

Federation by the right to command.

The Crown Prince of Nyzan was chosen by two prime requisites being met. First, he must be the smartest in all his great federation. This factor was arrived at by their extremely advanced computer culture. The second requirement was one faced in the circle of death. This circle could be entered by any male accepted by the computer. And this quiet man had ruled for over 200 years!

Our Federation had much second-hand information on this Older-than-Man Dynasty. And here I was, a lowly captain of a starprobe, sitting with the most single important being in all the charted universe.

"The cat seems to have your tongue. Or is it us cats that have it?" Nhioby laughed gaily. Suddenly a frown crossed her smooth brow. "They come my Lord!" she whispered.

Without rising from his seat Kookerman reached across the table and slipped two fingers into my belt, with an effortless swing of his arm he hurled me up into the loft. A ten foot flicking of a hundred and sixty pounds. And from a sitting position. It left me with no doubt as to his incredible story. Absolutely no doubt remained that Kookerman the brain damaged, was in fact the Crown Prince Nyzarbad. And Nhioby was his Queen. If I could just get this news to the Federation the stranglehold now being applied to my Federation would be ended.

Nhark was temporarily at peace but of all the planets in the known Universe. Nhark was the most war-like. It would be a great joy for all on Nhark to once more have a foe. With great joy would the Nharks assume the task of freeing their queen and solving this problem of the evil Singers.

Just a single message would save the Free Federation. The Federation was not born in violence nor had it ever become one of violent power. The Federation's great strength was one of empathy. Nothing more!

And I had the answer to its greatest threat. How to get that information to the Federation?

I peeked down between the small space in the loft floor.

Four single-qued Grunts sat at a table by the door and ordered hot kakleberry. Bulbus and Breezy came in and sat at the next table to the Grunts. They ordered a pitcher of Kakleberry. All the time making loud remarks about warriors who only wore a single carry-me-away.

The Grunts ignored them, but their eyes were busy elsewhere. They were looking for something

definite, and were not to be
sidetracked by the taunts of two
aggravating boys. They had been
well briefed and would not start
any foolish personal fighting.

They knew that to do so would be
to get the kiss of death from a
Singer. They were here for a
purpose, and would respond to
nothing other than their orders.

"Bulbus! Breezy! Leave these good
folk be," Kookerman ordered
quietly in a small voice that
carried just far enough.

Kookerman raised his glass in
salute to the Grunts. They raised
theirs, returning the salute,
grunting in satisfaction.

"Be you the Grodatt known as
Minnileaf?" asked a Grunt. His
three companions all locking their
dead eyes on Dilbo who sat still
as a mouse. It seemed to me that
Dilbo was actually paralyzed by
their combined dead eyes holding

him as a mouse in the presence of four terrible snakes.

"Whether this fine little Grodatt is Minnileaf, Wholeleaf, or six-leafs. What can it mean to you fine warriors?" Kookerman smiled without showing a single tooth.

"Our business be our business and not for the like of you to be questioning. And who be you?" leered the largest of the Grunts, showing his disdain with a small laugh.

"Laugh as you please. But do it ever so quietly," came a quiet, almost hissing reply as Kookerman smiled at the Grunts. A loud coarse guffaw from the foursome, was his reply.

"Beware! Before your lack of respect finds you in a position that will be no laughing matter. Life is like sweet wine. If you have it, sip it quietly, else it is taken away from you."

The Windwalkers Of Xambic

"What is this mad fool yapping about?" the leader of the Grunts asked his cohorts.

"This mad fool is warning you of the coming," the grinning Nhioby laughed without humor. It sent a chill through me and it wasn't directed at me.

"The coming?" asked the Grunt.

"Yes the coming of the end. Your end!" snapped Nhioby.

"Another mad fool." loudly replied the Grunt.

Before the words had left the mouth of the Grunt, Kookerman was at their table. "Gentlemen you are on the precipice of oblivion. Beware of the harbinger of the endless void."

The four Grunts roared in laughter.

"We mean to take the stinkin little Grodatt and you had better be gone before we take you, you mad fool." a Grunt said, reaching up to put his massive hand in Kookerman's face and shove him away from the table. Calmly and without effort Kookerman's long sinewy hand grasped the thick wrist of the Grunt and held it gently yet firm enough that the Grunt could not release it.

"You're not listening! I'm trying to save your eternal lives from the reaper. Pay attention!" Kookerman whispered.

Four flint daggers appeared from under cloaks.

Each dagger was driven hard at the eyes of Kookerman. Without effort and with what looked to be without even having moved. Kookerman stepped back from the table.

"You are now at the gate of the Final Reaper. Leave my presence or be no more!" came the mocking voice without threat. Just a simple statement.

The Windwalkers Of Xambic

"We take the Grodatt and the one hiding above us. We take them alive and we leave you gurgling in your blood. Fool!" came the angry reply from the leader of the loathsome Grunts.

"My Lord Nyzarbad. I tire of you toying with these insignificant creatures. Kill them or whatever, but rid me of their loud and loathsome presence," Nhioby ordered.

"Nyzarbad!" the four Grunts whispered in a single voice.

"My lovely. Why do you seek the lives of these poor things?"

"Now that they know of my identity they can no longer be allowed to leave. And we have no means of keeping them in captivity."

"Woman you cause me concern. And unneeded concern born of mischief. What say you my love?" Kookerman asked Nhioby.

"Is this a plea for clemency?" Nhioby purred. "Aye it is," Kookerman muttered.

"Faces on the floor swine and you will live to be a nuisance. Disobey and you surely meet the reaper." Nhioby said, with great darkness in her small voice. Four bodies fell to the ground with their heads pressed tightly to the floor in fear.

"So be it," Nhioby said her eyes rolling inward. A soft glow emanated from her now-golden orbs sending spasms through the four on the floor. The foursome collapsed.

"Your wish is my command. My Lord." Nhioby said.

"Woman you sometimes try my patience," Kookerman said, laughing good naturedly at his mate.

"And sometimes you try mine, my love," Nhioby said, smiling.

"Marples come down!" Kookerman ordered.

I could not believe my ears. How could this man know who I was the descendant of? How could a Prince of Nyzan even know of the existence of an insignificant starprober? Why would he expose his identity to this tavern of Grodatts?

"Fear not for us little one. Before we leave all memories will be washed clean of what has transpired," came a very strong inner-voice that hurt very little as opposed to the extreme pain of previous invasions of my mind.

"Nhioby?" I stammered. Looking to the face of the beautiful, but frightening queen of Nhark.

"Do not fear." came the soft response-- unsaid but firm.

"It doesn't hurt. Yet when I entered the tavern it did. How can that be?" I asked.

"You rejected the mindlink before." Nhioby said.

"And I didn't this time?" I asked aloud.

"Apparently not." Nhioby said smiling wickedly.

"Leave be!" Kookerman ordered.

"Your whim is my command. My Lord," Nhioby said quietly.

"Now we must leave. Bulbus! Breezy!" The twins entered carrying trade-bags.

"Nhioby. It is time." Kookerman ordered sternly. Vertigo and nausea overcame me. Then darkness.

AN AIRFOLK ATTACK

I lay on the floor. A floor that was madly spinning under me. In terror I clawed at the floor. Then Nothingness! I came to in a bed upstairs. "What happened?"

"You been introduced to dem thieven traders," Mildleaf the Mouser said from the next bed.

"Where is Dilbo?" I asked.

"Dilbo woke up bout a click gone by. You slept good. Someday we gonna do sumting bout dem damn thieven boogers!"

"How did they do it?" I asked, already knowing the answer.

"They uses sleep dust. Everyone knows that. Someday we stop them. Even the Singers tryna catch dem. Spideys be offerin reward for capturing dem traders. We been

107

setting traps, but den we forget about where traps be set. Last month we caught Boozy twice!" Mildleaf chuckled good naturedly.

"Why do the Singers want them?" I asked, but wondering if the Grodatts had any idea.

"They doesn't like them," Mildleaf replied, and I could tell by his simple answer that not liking them was reason enough for the Singers. But did the Singers have any idea of their true identities I wondered, but kept my thoughts to myself.

It was obvious that the Grodatts had no idea of the true identities of the traders. I knew even Dilbo thought of them as nothing more than thieves. Did Winnie Minniplant know the truth? And if she did why keep it a secret from her son?

A dull booming came from the great bent thumb of a mountain.

"What is that?" I asked Mildleaf
the Mouser.

"Be the warning of Mhyn. Come."
Mildleaf said.

Outside, in the bright light a dry
breeze was whisking three ragged
balloons along. As each shaggy
balloon drifted over the village,
shouts were exchanged between
those on the ground, and those in
the balloons. The balloons drifted
over the village and smacked into
the great bent thumb of a mountain
known as Mhyn Mountain completely
destroying the balloons.

"What kind of an attack was that?"
I asked Mildleaf.

Full scale. Three airbags. Can't
get serioser'n dat."

"But nobody was hurt," I argued.

"Dey made big threats. Fer sure."
Mildleaf replied.

"Look, their bags are flattened
out against the mountain. How can

they do anything now?" I asked Mildleaf.

"They just be showin da power. Three big bags be lots power fer sure," Mildleaf said, as if to a child.

"Can't be more power'n three baggers." Boozy Bentleaf put in, as if talking to a moron...

Soon the motley crew of Airbaggers came flopping and struggling down the glassy face of Mhyn Mountain.

"Now you see the power fer sure." Mildleaf said.

"Considerations are in order. Do you Grodatts agree?" the tallest of the approaching bean poles said, grinning.

"Most powerful war-party we be seeing" Boozy Bentleaf said, quietly to the Mouser.

"Keep quiet Boozy. Maybe dey hear you. Den they'll want da many extras." Mildleaf whispered.

The Windwalkers Of Xambic

Personally I couldn't understand where the threat was. All I could see was a pathetic group of filthy unarmed beanpoles.

Ican Grodatt being the Major-minor and the official voice of Grodatt addressed the motley group.

"Greetings Augustus Fung, you be outdoing self in having such a large n powerful airbagging under yer command. We here Grodatts be impressed. But why you attack in such force? For many times gone by, da treaty fer da peace be stood up by all. Why you now be attacking in such powerfulness?"

"We need more peep-weed. Little Airfolk are growing up, and are in need of the weed. We mean no harm to this illustrious group of gentlefolk but we have a deep need, not just a want, for more weed of the pipe. If you could just teach us to grow fwa-foo ourselves why we could all keep the peace without us having to

111

show our power." Augustus Fung said imperiously.

"Would teach you, but you would never learn. Teaching is not problem. Only a Grodatt be able to learn bout peep-weed."

"You are inferring that we are too stupid to learn something as basic as growing a weed?" challenged Fung.

"Not tellin bout stupid fer you just tellin dat growin the fine leaf of the Longbottom be onliest fer Grodatts to do." Ican of the Grodatts explained.

"Then you are saying we are not as good as Grodatts?" Scram, the second in command and Captain of his very own balloon, asked, with anger in his squeaky voice.

"Not talkin bout smart, ner not smart. Talkin bout grownin the fwa-foo. Yer not be a Grodatt ...."

The Windwalkers Of Xambic

"What the hell has being a Grodatt got to do with growing a simple gol damned weed?" the third captain piped in, completely confusing and upsetting the Grodatt.

Ican was confused by the Airbaggers talking out of turn. Not to listen patiently to everything said by an opponent before replying, was an unforgivable breach in Protocol of War as laid down in the Great Charter of Mhyn Mountain.

"Do you as the Spokesperson for all of Grodatt agree to teach us how to grow the plant? Specifically the fwa-foo plant?" a good natured Airbagger asked in a totally innocent and friendly manner.

Ahh my good fren, leKlunc, As a person you be asking, or is as a officer of Airbagg?"

"Just asking as a friend in need to a friend with weed."

"Your Majo-minor -- Might I speak?" Dilbo asked Ican.

Dilbo had moved up to the Airbagger known as leKlunc and was eyeball to belt with leKlunc. LeKlunc dropped to his knees and sat back on his heels. Now he was on and equal eyeballing with Dilbo.

"Permission be yers." Ican said petulantly, for he wanted this peace treaty to be remembered as his treaty with no interfering but he had no choice as open speech for all to hear was the only way for a Grodatt.

"If you want to learn the way of the weed. I will teach you. You do want to learn to grow... Don't you?" Dilbo asked.

"You are talkin' might strange for a Grodatt." LeKlunc said, peering suspiciously at Dilbo.

"Yes. I suppose so but I am tired of talking like an imbecile and my

114

good friend Tink tells me I have
nothing to be ashamed of and no
reason to pretend to be other than
I am..."

"And what is it you are?" asked
leKlunc with a grin. "And who is
your good friend Tink?" he
laughed.

"He is standing right behind you,
ask him yourself." Dilbo Minnileaf
told the friendly Airbagger.

At this point I stepped around
into LeKluncs field of vision and
sat down beside him smiling my
most reassuring teeth-loaded-
smile. This was my best
negotiating face.

"Aha! A Grodatt that is not a
Grodatt." Augustus Fung said,
sitting down to join our little
circle. Soon the circle was
anything but little, as all the
Airbaggers and Grodatts moved in
to form a circle.

Why do I feel that you are all forming a circle around me?" I asked nobody in particular.

"If you're not an Airbagger and you're not. And if you're not a Grodatt and I think you are not.. Then who are you? And why are you living here under the noses of the damn spiders? In very great danger. I might say!" Augustus Fung challenged.

"Isn't all of Grodatt in danger?" I replied.

"Course not. Look around there must be at least five comalongs in this gathering alone. Who would consider any form of violence in the presence of a comalong?" Fung asked.

"It's true Tink, only a fool bent on self-destruction would consider any violence toward one of us Grodatts," Dilbo answered the huge captain but his eyes were on me.

"What of the soldiers in the Wild Piggoty Inn?" I challenged.

"They were especially not dangerous to us Grodatts. For they work directly for the Singers, and no spider would ever consider any harm to any Grodatt," Dilbo said.

"Why would they not harm a Grodatt?" I asked.

"Only we can grow the fwa-foo and without it they are stranded here, exactly as you are and all the others who have come before." Dilbo Minnileaf said. All the crowd nodded their heads in silent agreement.

"Then I am the only one in any danger?" I asked, already knowing the answer.

"Oh. I suppose all of us on Xambic are in some sort of danger, except the Grodatts of course," LeKlunc said.

"And we'd be in very serious danger if the Singers ever figure

a way to grow the fwa-foo." Dilbo
said simply.

"This little talk has cleared up
any ideas that we Airbaggers have
had about learning the secret of
fwa-foo. Does anyone differ with
me?" Fung asked his cohorts. All
agreed that whatever the secret to
the growing of fwa-foo was, it was
not so much a secret as it was a
way of doing that could only be
done by a Grodatt. They all
accepted this and then set about
negotiating a trading for more
fwa-foo.

It was quickly made clear to me
why the Grodatts had developed
such a benevolent nature. They had
absolutely no enemies and anyone
even considering violence against
them would have to answer to one
of the ever present comalongs.

I could see why Mildleaf the
Mouser was all that was required
in the way of a police force.
Actually I could not see any

reason for even his pretending to be a policing agent. It turned out that the threat that had been implied by the Airbaggers was to drop a salt compound on the garden from the three airbags, however it was only a threat and I soon realized a not very serious one.

It just turned out to be a formality in the greater game of horse-trading for the valued plant. Neither the Airfolks nor the Grodatts took any of it to mean any more than amusing foreplay that would later be followed with the real act of trading, which they were now doing in earnest.

But the Singers had also seen the airbags drifting in low over the village and they knew this to be foreplay for the gentle art of trading. And the Singers were having none of it. The fwa-foo was all theirs by right of might and even the smallest leaf being traded elsewhere, was a leaf that they would not get. And their need was already much greater than their present supply.

Kaboom-- kaboom-- kaboom came a deep threatening dinning from the swampy Singer camp. Even the Grodatts who were in no danger from the foul Singers, shuddered.

TINK MEETS THE SINGERS

Out of the glimmering came a smell
of burning flesh drifting up from
the dreaded Singer camp. The
glimmering that was too bright to
see into, seemed to lose a little
of its eerie brilliance right over
the 666 Tetrahedron. Soon, the
reason for the change in the
glimmering web could be seen by
all.

A small glimmering broke loose
from the main web.

"What is happening?" I asked
Dilbo.

"Someone is being paid a rare
compliment," Dilbo said, looking
from one face to the next of the
three Airbag captains.

"Don't be looking at me!" Augustus
Fung yelled, visibly shaken at the

sight of the obscene glimmering
that was moving away from the
Singer camp.

"Not afraid of a singer are you?"
asked Dilbo innocently.

"Not a point of being afraid. It's
a point of not being stupid and
suicidal. Those that had not the
good sense to respect the evil of
a Singer are not with us anymore.
I say that caution is the smartest
part of valor, and when it comes
to dealing with Singers – I'm for
showing my smartest of smarts."

"Anyone think I'm a coward?" Fung
said, looking very close into the
faces of all present, but
especially into the face of
LeKlunk. LeKlunk only grinned
innocently.

Kaboom-- kaboom-- kaboom, came the
reverberations that could be felt
to the bone. And I noticed that I
was not the only one that
shuddered each time the dreadful
reverberation penetrated each and

every one of us present. Even the
stalwart comalongs ran around in
circles, all the time whimpering.

"It is a great respect they pay
you Tink, never have they come for
anyone before," Dilbo said,
looking at me with great brown
eye, loaded with fear for me.
Regardless of what else was to
happen, I knew that Dilbo was
truly my friend.

The sun was just on the horizon,
and a flat red sky added to the
depression and fear that had
overtaken this happy group of
children-like people.

"I'm for fighting the filthy
things... Who's with me?" LeKlunc
said with fear and anger in his
strong voice.

I was forced to revaluate my
previous opinion about this
Airbagger. For, in spite of his
jovial, "I'm ok, and who cares
about you?" attitude. He had a

very deep concern about the Singers.

"We don't stick together, they'll take us one at a time. Right now they want Tinkerman, and if we let him stand alone today, tomorrow, it might just be you, or you, or you." LeKlunc said, pointing to his cohorts at random. "What say you?"

"Ah, you know we'll back you, right boys?" came the reply from Fung, as he put his arm around the shoulder of his number one captain. "Loosen Uup Buuuudy!" Fung laughed, but with a mirthless fright filled voice, devoid of conviction.

"Can't loosen up, but I'm sticking with the little guy," leKlunc said, as he came over and sat beside Dilbo and me.

Scram and Fung came over to join us. The Grodatts gathered around me in a tight circle. Each little body forming a living wall between

me and the horror that was
approaching.

As the glimmering proceeded
through the now empty village,
darkness was upon us. Only the
evil glimmering emanating from the
Singers gave light to the night.
It would have been, just another
night but with the horror of the
unknown and the penetrating of the
drumming, this normal dark became
a place of terror.

"We been through thick and thin
with you Captain," came a
frightened voice from one of the
Airbaggers.

"And now?" Augustus Fung
challenged, rising to his feet.

"Well the crew wants no fight with
these spiders. We figure to take
care of our own, but..." And the
man looked to the crew for
support. To a man, they looked to
the sand.

"Can't blame them Captain. I'm not their problem."

"Ahhh... I'm not blaming the weak rascals. Just wondering if it was Scram, or LeKlunc, or me, what then? Would they stay? Or would they leave their Captain to fend for himself. I"m not blaming any of them, but I'm not feeling very good either. You boys had better be going-- If that's to be your decision."

To a man the Airfolk sat down, hating and loving their leader with a dreading.

"Knew you to be good men. Every man-jack of ya." Fung said proudly, tears forming in his crazy eyes. "Shiiit." he said, sitting down beside "LeKlunc.

"Nothin but an old mother hen." LeKlunc laughed.

The night was not as dark as on many planets, because of the light supplied by the many moons that rotated high overhead. But, it was dark enough to suit this particular gathering.

Around the edge of the last hut in the village the glimmering came. Now it could be seen more in perspective for what it really was, and that was, two four-wheeled carts, that were pushed-pulled-tugged by a horde of armed Grunts. Each Grunt had a great ebonwood sword in one hand, and used the other to move the heavy ebonwood cart he was attached to.

"Two Singers," Dilbo said, in awe.

"Never seen one away from the group, now I see two. They surely mean business with you Tink." Scram said breaking his normal silence.

As the glimmering moved ever so carefully and slowly towards us not a body moved. It was as if a great snake had raised its hypnotic head, and here we sat

waiting our death in abject
terror.

"Aaaayyyaaaahhh," came the scream
of rage from LeKlunc, as he leaped
to his feet and with a bound borne
of superhuman fear, with a single
effortless leap, LeKlunc cleared
the Grodatts and headed for the
glimmering, with a scream in his
throat, and a berserking in his
every muscle.

The glimmering procession stopped,
and a directional glow reached out
to close the gap between the
almost flying LeKlunc and the
Singers. Whatever the nature of
the glowing, it had no viewable
effect on LeKlunc, as he closed
the gap without a lessening in his
mad drive for a Singer. LeKlunc
had reached behind his back and
pulled out two evil looking
sneems.

The carts were about fifty feet
apart. As LeKlunc all but flew at
the closest cart, half the Grunts

came forth to challenge. The
fighting was the fiercest that
I've ever been present to view. I
could only view what was happening
in an impotent rage, as my very
essence as a being was held fast
by a power greater than my own
will. Somehow, I knew this was
also the case of all the Grodatts
as well. I felt their empathetic
locking and unlocking with one
another to strengthen and console,
but even this large group had not
enough ergs to escape the tractor
power of a single Singer at close
range.

Dead Grunts lay everywhere. The
cart itself was a sizzling,
smoking thing that sent an acrid
blue-green cloud overhead. Then
the cart itself broke into flames,
and burned with a crackling that
lit up the whole area. It was
bright as day, with only a
terrible stench to make a
difference. With the loss of the
one cart, and the mysterious

disappearance of its dreadful occupant, the Grunts attached to it fell back to protect the other cart and its two-ton occupant.

From out in the desert could be heard the inhuman screams of a mind given over to madness, and occasionally a scream of a Grunt hunted down by that mad thing in the night. I shuddered, as I knew that mad thing was just a few minutes ago sitting next to me in the form of LeKlunc.

I looked to Augustus for an answer.

"It's his way. He's a Berserker from Nhark." was Augustus' simple reply. Knowing of the fierce madness of the warriors from Nhark, I actually felt sorry for the Grunts that he hunted in the dark. But not too sorry, for a group still remained around the other Singer.

"What happened to the spider?" I asked Dilbo.

"It would appear that she couldn't hold on to the Nhark war madness, so she fled to the safety of her camp," Dilbo said.

I looked up to see if any of the other Airbaggers were transported by the Nhark madness, but saw to my concern that whatever they had been transported by under the confusion of LeKlunc's attack had been to transport them out of the situation. Only Scram and Augustus Fung remained.

"How come only LeKlunc attacked?" I asked Fung.

"LeKlunc is the only Nhark in our group, most of the time we wish he wasn't, but right now I wish we were all Nharks."

"How come you and Scram didn't flee?" I asked.

"Some things a man can't do and still be a man." Scram put in with deep feeling in his voice.

"What will happen to LeKlunc?"I asked, worried for the safety of the gentle-but-mad warrior.

"He'll hunt those Grunts down, then he'll collapse and sleep for a week. In a week or two he'll stumble into camp with a sheepish grin on his face, and we'll have silly old LeKlunc around again until he short-circuits again," Fung said.

As the remaining singer was brought forward by her entourage of dolt-Grunts, the main body of Airbaggers fled into the dark of the desert. And I now had freedom to move as well. Apparently this group was too large for one Singer to hold onto, and because it took two Singers to control me, my life was safe.

"Grodatts Flee!" came a wet, gasping voice from the huge four wheeled cart. All the remaining Grunts had formed a full circle around the Singer. She sat

motionless in the ebon cart. Only
her single multifaceted eye had
any sign of life. It glistened
with a malevolence. Now that the
cart was close enough for us all
to see her in all her two tons of
horror, we could see why she
needed a cart.

Her great walking-legs had all
atrophied from generations of none
use. Around the cart itself, she
was attended by six male spiders.
Each little frightened creature
would stroke the great soggy
thing, only for her to try and
catch them with her small feeding
arms, but with great speed, and
fear, three of the 40 pound near
skeletons would keep her busy
trying to grab and eat them, while
the remaining three would rush in
and caress her from her blind
side.

As she slowly rotated her massive
eye, they would scurry away, and
the other three would rush in, in

fear, and stroke and rub her ghastly body. This continued for over a click, while the Grodatts sat hypnotized, still paralyzed.

I knew that I could flee at any time, and felt only curiosity about this great ghoulish slab of slime, and her hairy little suitors. I knew that if I moved a hair, she would realize I had the volition of movement. And the fact that she was unable to read me clearly, or even at all, was my only defense. And it was a wild card I would not use until I really had no choice left.

"How are all my little friends?" came a wet, sickly voice from the great mound of pulsating flesh.

Not a Grodatt replied.

"Dilbo. Will you not answer me? Surely you have the courage to answer a helpless old woman."

With the word woman, on those flabby lips, the body of Grodatts

134

shuddered as a single body. This caused a high pitched giggling from the six males, who were busy with their ghoulish courting of this malevolent thing.

"If Dilbo don' talk ... Not his place... Ican Grodatt be der voice a all us here Grodatts," Ican said, with great fear in his small voice.

"Ahhhh! A Grodatt with courage. Come forth that I may see you the better, my little champion of Grodatt."

Ican sat as if in a coma. All the other Grodatts, and the Airbaggers were also unable to move. I knew I was the only one not caught by the power of this hideous creature. And I had a feeling that the Singer knew I was uncontrolled. What I was not sure of was whether she was toying with me, or could it be possible that she was unable to get a fix on me?

Soon my unanswered question was answered.

"Amongst you foolish little growers is an earthling. Give him to me, and you will be released from my presence. Disobey and I will eat two of you-- right here. And right now! Do you understand? Fools!"

The Grodatts sat frozen in terror, yet not a word was spoken, and I knew the Singer had left them with that one function. But not an utterance. Even the horny little male spiders could feel the terror she was driving into the tiny Grodatts, and they all backed away from her in temporary fear.

Without a word being spoken, four of the Grunts moved woodenly forward and selected two children from the circle protecting me.

"You've made your point," I said, getting to my feet.

The Windwalkers Of Xambic

With the same wooden-controled-by movement as before, the Grunts released the children. The children collapsed to the sand.

"Release your grip on the Grodatts, and I'll come to you."

"NO ... No ... Noo ..." came the reply from the seated Grodatts.

"Very touching. And I might admit ... of courage. Come closer, and not a gardener will I eat. At least not this night," the evil ghoul said, voice heavy with sick humor.

"Release the Grodatts, and I'll come forward in peace. Hold them for another second, and I'll test the ability of your guard, and I think a guard not able to stand the attack of a single Nhark-warrior, will not enjoy what I have in store for them."

"And you are a warrior too? My, my. My sisters and I have speculated whether you could be just a Probe captain, or could you have been in fact instructed to land, even as that fool next to you. Stand up Scram and come forward with this tiny fool."

"Release the Grodatts! Release them now. For in the name of the RhaEve, I Marples Tinkerman will have your slimy hide."

"Marples Tinkerman? You expect me to believe you are the same Marples that walked with the RhaEve of Rha?"

"Believe what you like. But your life rides on your having an understanding of what has gone before," I said, removing my two glassicate sneems from under my jacket.

I started forward, toward the ugly beast. My directive had been to take no life, however, according to my interpretation of life, I wasn't about to take a life. My directive had no clauses about defending myself against vermin.

"Stooop!" Came an ear splitting shriek from the Singer.

I stopped. "Release the Grodatts."

"First a few questions. Questions, only the Marples who walked with a living god would know the answers to."

"Fair enough."

"What was the name of the Old One who lived in the One Tree?"

"The Old One never lived in a tree, it lived in a well, and it was not one, rather it was part of a group-being, an energy group-being that lived apart, yet connected to itself."

"What... did live in The Tree?" asked the Singer, with less mockery in her voice.

"Something you will never want to meet," I said, hoping I was projecting my most suggestive, and threatening laugh.

"You are not answering me."

"I think I just have, and I think you know why you are unable to control me. For I have walked with the RhaEve, and I have sat with my feet in the killing lake for thousands of years." I could see that the ghoulish creature was visibly shaken by my words, and the fact she knew that she had no control over me.

"The lake. Name the lake," the Singer said, with a tremor.

"Rhadium-da-dum-da-dum ... R-H-A-D-1-U-M ..." I spelled.

"Enough!" the ghoul shrieked, in rage and terror.

"Let my people go," I said, not being able to miss the chance to ham-it-up. And I could see that this little touch of theatrics was the final straw. The Singers had unhealthy interests in the histories of all of their enemies. And I knew that only a Singer would know this phrase. Actually, only a Singer, or someone who was over four thousand years old.

"Your people are free." the Singer shuddered. "But this is far from the end of it."

"Next time you will have the Khrx guard I suppose."

"No need to suppose. We have a stalemate right now, but as soon as my sister has recovered. You will meet our Khrx, and even if you are Marples, so what!"

"All this for a little peep weed," I said.

"It is our future. And if these fools don't start producing it in quantity. They will cease to exist. It is all just a matter of time, my small warrior. You and I have endless time, and sooner or later, the Khrx will find you. And when they do, I'll personally eat your tiny little bones."

Having nothing more to say, the horde of Grunts moved their master back to the camp.

"Well it looks like this round goes to the good guys," Dilbo said, shaking my hand. Every Grodatt in the still protective circle, formed a line. Every Grodatt came forward and touched their head to the heads of us three who had remained.

"Scram. All this time you have let me believe you to be an empty headed trader, who purposely landed here, just for the purpose of trade. Can there be more to you? Why would a Singer want you? A mere Freebooter?" Augustus Fung asked.

"Who can understand a Singer's wants?" replied Scram, innocently. But he had convinced Augustus of nothing.

"You are very old?" asked Dilbo.

"Nah, I was just bluffing."

"How do you account for knowing of the happenings on Rha?"

"Oh, that was just bogus information I made up. No one knows if there really is a Marples Tinkerman that walked with the RhaEve. It is a story that goes back over four thousand years. Personally, I think it is a fable created by the federation in its infancy. To link it with a great-good-power, would have given it credibility in its infancy."

"That being the case. Why is it still believed today?"

"Some myths are slow in dying, Dilbo." I said laughing and punching Dilbo on the arm.

"Hmmmpph." Dilbo muttered. "What is your true name then?" Dilbo challenged.

"Oh my name is really Marples Tinkerman. But that's where it starts and ends," I said, looking into Dilbo's trusting eyes with my best, most-honest pose.

"Not good to lie to your brothers and sisters. And just in case you missed the significance of the honor you and Scram... And Fung have been shown. The whole village has accepted you three as members to this village. This honor has never been shown to an outsider before."

"Never?" I challenged.

"Well almost never. Only my mother has been accepted as an outsider, and if you are wanting the real truth. Then it's the village itself that are outsiders, and Mom who is the only person who really belongs. But that's a matter of opinion."

"Just keeping you as honest as you are keeping me."

We both laughed.

The villagers had all gone to the Mhyn. And Fung had slipped off in

144

search of his cowardly crew. Only Scram and Dilbo and I remained to watch the evil procession returning to the Glimmering.

"There'll be an ugly night in the swamp for the poor Grunts." Scram said, quietly.

"Poor Grunts?" Dilbo said, looking carefully at Scram.

"You had better get back to the security of Mhyn." I said to my good and valiant friend.

ON THE RUN

I headed into the desert with only
one thought in mind, and that
thought was to find The Crown
Prince Nyzerbad. Little did I know
how difficult this was going to
be.

"Mind if I tag along?" Scram said,
as if I would be doing him a
favor.

"I'm the one without a clue how to
make it on this weird planet.
Somehow I think I should be asking
if I could tag along with you," I
replied, letting him know that he
wasn't fooling me for a second.

"Don't you trust me?" Scram said,
feigning hurt.

"Don't pretend to feel insulted.
You and I know that you are a
whole lot more than you seem,

146

otherwise you would have fled with all the other scumbaggers."

"Airbaggers" he corrected.

"Whatever." I replied.

"What have you in mind for slowing down the Singers?" Scram asked.

"I have only one objective on this planet. And that is to get off it. Once I get in touch with the Federation, these spiders will be properly taken care of. So much for what I am up to. What directive could cause you to purposely land here?"

"Possibly the same directive that brought you here," Scram said all the time watching me for the slightest facial, or body language, to indicate what I was not telling.

"It wasn't a directive that brought me down. Splashing down here was a miscalculation on my part."

"Seems hard to believe that one so old could make such a simple miscalculation."

"Whoever you really are, Scram, and why you have decided to be my buddy, leaves me to wonder about you ... Far too much ... Unless you can tell me how you are able to read body-language so expertly, and why you are interested in me. And what you are really up to... I think we better part company, while I still have good feelings about you."

"I assure you I am both unarmed and anything but dangerous, but I am following a prime directive from my Federation ..."

"And what Federation would that be?" I cut in.

Scram stopped, and turned to face me.

"I'm not your enemy Marples Tinkerman," he said sincerely.

"No, I don't think you are. I
don't think you are the enemy to
anyone. I don't believe you are
even an enemy of the Singers. Are
you an enemy to the spiders?" I
challenged.

"No I am not," Scram replied in a
small voice.

"Well... Maybe this is a start.
Could even be the first total
honest statement from you."

"Then you will reconsider about
traveling together?"

"Might as well. We have a saying
on my planet, that it is wise to
keep your friends close to you,
and those that may be your
enemies-- even closer."

"I think you mean, those that are
your enemies, not those that may
be," Scram corrected.

"No I mean those that may be, for
I don't agree with the original
thought. I like to keep my enemies

a long way off. Like in another Galaxy."

"Well, then it appears as if we have both afforded the other a very small piece of honesty. And that is a start."

"Yes. I suppose it is something." I replied.

And with this small honesty and great doubt about each other, we headed into the barren, cold, dark, away from the friendship of the Grodatts, and away from the dreadful Singers. I felt guilty of leaving the Grodatts at the mercy of the spiders, but knew that in order to help, I was going to need help myself.

We walked until first light, trying to put as many miles between the Singers and ourselves, before the weakened Singer recovered full power. Then I knew they would be looking for me with a vengeance. They knew they had control over the game they were playing, and they knew I was a wild card that meant them no good. In truth. That's all I was-- a wild card with no identity or power of my own. All I had going for me, was the fact that I could not be predicted, and that fact alone was reason for the spiders to throw all their energy into stopping me, before I started an epidemic of wild cards for them to have to contend with.

Scram and I traveled for three days, only sleeping a few clicks each night. We knew that the Singers could not project themselves into an area where they had not previously been in the Physical sense. Until they had a chance to bring in their dreaded Khrx, we were in no danger.

The fourth day out Scram disappeared while I slept.

A hot breeze blew in along the white dunes, but I could smell the fragrance of the sea. Being alone

was no problem, but being alone
without water was a very real
problem. However, I had a clear
picture of this strange planet
firmly etched in my mind from the
numerous orbits I'd made while
still on my starprobe.

I knew the band ran entirely
around the planet in what could be
considered an East-West
coordinate. The band was uniform
in its twenty mile wide sand strip
that encircled the equator. So I
knew that even if I was in the
absolute center of this band--
life giving water could be never
more than 10 miles away.

Given that the planet tilted just
slightly towards its sun in its
orbiting, I decided that I would
designate this direction as being
North on this ovate spheroid known
as Xambic. That being the case,
the twenty mile wide band of land
that encircled the water ball must

be considered to be East-West
oriented.

While this was just my means of
keeping my head organized in
regard to direction on Xambic, the
overall picture of galactic
Navigation is at the best merely
dependent on a set of arbitrary
directions and values, that are
only directional in the sense of
being relative to a known set of
coordinates. Coordinates that a
navigator has given man made
symbols to. Navigation was really
less complicated on Xambic than in
any space or planet I'd ever
encountered. On Xambic, even a
child could never be lost.

And I was far from a child. I
walked east for three miles
following the freshwater sea. Each
morning I would get up long before
the sun came up, bury my fire, and
head east, always keeping to the
shoreline.

The fifth mile I knew I was being followed.

Two clicks before sunset, I set about lensing my evening fire, just before the sun went down. If I let the light get too low, then, even the powerful single lens on a thong that all Starprobers wore, would fail to get my evening cookfire going.

With a small smokeless fire burning at waterside, and a mess of pink shrimp-like crustaceans simmering in a cocata pod. I set about shearing an armful of cocata fronds for my bed.

KOOKERMAN

"Nice fire." came a whisper from behind the clump of cocata trees.

"Soup's on. Or would you rather whisper at me from the dark?" I asked, not bothering to turn and face the intruder.

"Careless makes for a short life. How could you have lived so long?" came the soft reply.

"I've been tracking you ever since you left the village with the spy. I could have killed you any time. How can one so careless live so long?" came the familiar whisper.

"Actually I've been tracking you." I said.

"You've been tracking me? Don't talk nonsense."

"Certainly I've been tracking you. I just figured to keep looking for you until you decided to find me."

"That makes no sense."

"Sense or not... You are here. Can you dispute this?"

"I am beginning to doubt that you are the same Marples Tinkerman that walked on Rha with the RhaEve?"

"I never made any statement that I was." I chuckled"

"No. I suppose not... But if you are, why this game?" Nyzerbad asked, stepping into view.

"Not really a game. I have just been making sure that you are alone, and you are. And I wanted you within the range of my sneems, just in case you were not who I believed you to be."

"And?"

"You are alive, so you must be who I expected."

The Windwalkers Of Xambic

"Do you expect me to believe that you have been aware of my presence for miles, and that you were in no danger, and are in fact in none ... Now?" hissed Nyzerbad.

"From where I'm sitting you have walked into a trap, not sprung one. However, this is a moot point, as we have the same objectives and enemies."

"Yes... Our enemies are the same, but as to our objectives, that we must discuss, and as to who is in whose trap. Prove what you say, and I'll not doubt you again," Nyzerbad replied.

"I have no intentions of killing you just to prove that it can be done, but I will share my soup, and shortly I may prove that it is not always the hunted that is truly the prey."

"Wise words. If they are proven."

"What do you know of Marples?"

"I know that Marples has lived for over four thousand years as a troubleshooter for the Federation."

"So it is rumored, but you must know something that only the real Marlpes Tinkerman could know, or do."

"I know he is a master survivalist."

"Well, I'm surviving." I said with a grin.

"True. You are alive, however, I see that the question as to which Marples you really are... is about to answer itself."

From the small clump of cocata fronds a rippling in the sand could be seen, but only if one had the ability to see. The rippling was certainly a sandviper, and it was headed for me at an alarming speed. One bite was almost instant death. Nyzerbad just stood and grinned as the deadly ten foot snakemole made straight for me, now almost breaking sand.

"Your body heat may be your death, little one." Nyzerbad said not making a move to come to my aid. I sat totally motionless. I could see that Nyzerbad was completely locked into my scenario. His green-black eyes were glazed in fascination by my predicament ... As the rippling was upon me. I struck deep into the sand with my left hand, and at the same time sprung to my feet.

The viper was a small one, and I had almost grabbed it too far forward, almost too close to those terrible fangs of instant death. Without even looking at the evil thing, I lopped its vile head off, right at the eyes, then, I threw the thrashing body away from me without looking even once at what my hands were doing. Never for a second did I unlock my gaze from that of Nyzerbad.

"Very impressive." Nyzerbad said, a smile in his eyes.

Without a word I whirled the sneem. It buried itself deep in the sand at the feet of Nyzerbad. He still had not moved, merely standing there with the blue moonlight from the two overhead moons playing across his expressionless face. Nyzerbad never looked down at the second writhing sandviper that thrashed about his feet, with my sneem buried deep in its repulsive head.

"Also very impressive." he said, stooping, his eyes never looking to the thrashing viper, but with an effortless swoop of his large hand, he scooped up the viper, removed my sneem and cut off its evil head, all without taking his eyes from mine.

"I think your credentials are as represented," he said with a laugh, throwing my sneem handle first into the sand at my feet.

160

The Windwalkers Of Xambic

"And now, about the soup you offered, my little friend."

"And about objectives?" I asked.

"Yes, certainly about our very real objective," Nyzerbad said, with what I could tell was real concern. And if it was of concern to this strange, but capable warrior king, then, it was a very serious problem. And one that caused my first feeling of uncertainty since my landing. For, if it was a situation to cause concern for Nyzerbad, it was more than I had bargained for when accepting the mission.

"Do you have any standby probes? Or are you as stranded as you appear to be?" Nyzerbad asked, dipping into the steaming chowder with a large clam shell.

"My Federation knows of my disappearance, but I am without backup of any kind. I have hoped for another probe to come floating down. Then, I would expect the

Federation to have a better look at the situation. They might interpret a single probe's not reporting in to be an isolated case, but losing two Probes in the same sector is a situation totally unacceptable to the Federation."

"Then, you are alone?"

"Except for you, and your queen-- and LeKlunc," I said.

"Yes LeKlunc is my good queen's captain. He has infiltrated all the groups that Nhioby and I figure to be of some help against the Singers."

"After his open assault on the armed Grunts, his value as a spy is finished. That terrible display of destruction let the spiders know that they have at least one Nhark warrior to contend with. They will replace all the Grunts with Khrx."

"It's too bad that leKlunc had to break cover, but at the first sign of trouble it is to be expected that the damn spiders would bring in their Khrx. Have you ever faced a Khrx in battle?"

"Too often," I replied, with a shudder.

"I've heard it said that two of the filthy beasts are a match for a Nhark-warrior."

"I'd as soon not meet either in battle," I said.

"Nor I," Nyzerbad said, with a grin that could have meant he agreed, but then again, even his body language was under control, and I was quickly learning that I wasn't reading him.

Nyzerbad just sat on his heels and smiled.

"As I see it we have only the three of us against a soon to arrive horde of Khrx." I said.

"Never underestimate my lovely queen."

"No. I suppose that she is more than a match for a Khrx," I agreed.

"Nhioby is more than a match for a division of the filthy devils... If she is angered."

"Where is she?" I asked.

"She has felt the damage to LeKlunc, and is presently driving Bulbus and Breezy relentlessly* through the caves around Grodatt."

"Can't she just get a mindlink on him?" I asked.

"No. He is not responding to her summons. That's why she is concerned. If she was getting even the smallest response to her mindsweeps, she would not be concerned. Nhioby knows where he last emanated mindpatterns from in his berserking."

"And?"

"And nothing. That's the problem."

"Could he be dead?"

"No. Nhioby would detect the loss of his life."

"What about Scram?" I asked.

"Ah yes... Scram. Scram the stoic. Nhioby has given herself more than one headache trying to penetrate that fellow."

"He followed me into the dessert, then just disappeared."

"Do you know why he followed you?" Nyzerbad asked.

"No, but I think I know why he left."

"And that is?"

"I think he learned what he needed to know about me, and he was steadily becoming upset about my reading him."

"You could read him?" Nyzerbad asked, looking at me very carefully, almost with respect, I thought.

"Nhioby will be interested in talking to you about this. Of this I am very sure. Somehow I have a feeling she is more concerned with the presence of Scram than she is about being stranded on this stupid planet."

"Why not just ask her?"

"Just ask her?" Nyzerbad asked, then broke into a howling, growling, fit of laughter that caused me to move away from him.

"You have no idea of the nature of my Nhioby," Nyzerbad said, wiping the tears from his face with a wisp of silky cloth. He produced it from one of the many pockets in his great furry cloak.

"We can make plans when we return to my camp, but for now we should sleep, for even for Marples the Magnificent, the walk to my camp will be long and arduous."

I lay down on my frond bed, as I could envision my short legs being

166

forced to match the pace that I knew faced me.

"I have enough fronds for two humachees."

"No need, but thanks for the thought-- Little man." came the amused whisper. Nyzerbad moved out into the dunes, not unlike a wisp of black smoke that melted into the night, and I could imagine that with his great black hooded cloak, he really needed no heat from my little fire.

Also, I felt safer having him at a distance, not that I didn't trust him. I truly believed that he wanted to join forces, but... And then again, anyone sneaking up on me would get a terrible-black-surprise from out of the dunes.

I had difficulty in falling asleep. Although I was tired enough to sleep for a month, somehow the presence of Nyzerbad and Nhioby -- without their ships of war-- troubled me more than my immediate problem of reporting to the Federation. Why would they be in this sector unannounced, and without their Armada?

Had they really been drawn in? Or had Nioby purposely followed Scram down? And who and what the hell was Scram anyway? All these thoughts buzzed through my head as I drifted off into a deep sleep. Too deep...

CAPTURED

I could feel the sun on my face. Immediately, I sensed something was a wrong. Why was the sun well over the horizon, and I was still asleep?

Even half asleep I knew that Nyzerbad would not let me sleep this long out of the goodness of his heart. The fact that I had traveled for four days without sleep would have meant nothing to him. I knew that if he had driven himself for four days without sleep, I could expect no coddling, and I knew he would give none.

Where was he? I wondered, but not for long.

I opened both eves and sat up. To the east, to the west, and to the south-- Khrx. They were just mulling around, driving their long black glassite spears into the sand.

I ignored their presence, as they appeared to ignore mine. I went down to the water, stripped to the raw and had my first bath in a week. For want of soap I scrubbed my hands and feet with the sharp, white sand.

The Khrx gradually decreased their ring, all the time jabbing their long spears into the sand. I knew they hated water, so I knew they would not follow me into the water. This told me they were not interested in whether they took me alive or dead. The fact I was still alive meant they had some small reason for me being so.

Probably the Singers were interested in questioning me. But, in spite of orders, I knew it would take the smallest excuse for them to kill me. For they deeply enjoyed killing.

The Windwalkers Of Xambic

Not for one second did I even consider escaping in what appeared an unguarded direction. Methodically they jabbed their way towards me, not missing a square inch of sand with their long spears.

"Greetings," I said to the closest spider. It carried no spear, but another followed at a distance of ten feet, never getting closer, but never farther away. They moved as a unit. The follower carried not one long stabbing spear, it also carried six shorter throwing spears. The leader was no taller than any of the other evil creatures, but its head was larger, with a greater mouth. And with twice the venomous tuskage of its consorts. Even its stick-like arms were at least a foot longer. And from scaly boots to chitinous neck-armor it had sneems of various lengths inserted everywhere.

I knew it for what it was. Hopefully it was unaware of who I was. The fact that it let me try and escape, so that it could have the entertainment of killing me, was in my favor. I could only hope it mistook me for a Grodatt.

Soon I was to find out.

"Federator. Why do you not swim to safety?"

"Am I in danger?" I asked innocently.

"Do you think we are here to give you a birthday greeting? Do not underestimate us. Fool!"

"Truthfully I have no idea why you are here," I replied, as innocently as I could under the circumstances, without insulting its intelligence.

"Where is your companion?"

"My who?" I asked, projecting my blandest face.

172

The Windwalkers Of Xambic

All around me the ring had tightened to within scant feet of the Bhazz. As the Khrx approached their leader, they all dropped to one knee with their spear held high and their eyes lowered, never looking directly at the Bhazz, for it was the first-hatched, and by devouring most of its hatch-mates in the hatchling it had developed into just a little more than the other hatchlings. And a whole lot less in my way of looking at it, but their culture was older than Man, and who could say they were wrong.

I could loathe them, but even in my loathing I could not condemn their social order. Many ways made up the Galaxy, and all of them different. And we had not yet fully explored even our Galaxy. Never mind the infinite Galaxies too far for mankind to travel to.

While it was true that the RhaEve and the Old Ones traveled through all the Galaxies. Only they did so. And why they had left our Galaxy with only the Federation to keep the peace was not for mankind to know.

"You have entertained a guest here. Where is he?" the Bhazz demanded, its green, multi-faceted eyes unreadable to me. Even the hostility in its voice was unreadable.

My talent for reading began and ended with body language. And these bodies were nothing but sticks and chitin. Actually they were extremely easy to read, as they were always hostile, and would kill on the smallest provocation. This was more than I needed to know.

I knew that to lie outright would be an insult to this creature, and it would be an insult that would cost me my life. This much body language I was sure of.

"Noble Bhazz I did indeed entertain and feed a great black creature last night, but he left immediately after eating."

A great deal of chittering took place between the sixty Khrx, while the Bhazz listened to them, it never engaged in their chittering. Twice it twittered at a much higher Pitch to its spear bearer. The spear bearer lowered its head when replying with it's chitter.

Without understanding anything they said, I could feel the fear in its chitter. Only it was permitted to speak to the Bhazz it seemed, and it did so in fear. Already my small talent for reading was collecting data on these accursed creatures.

"It seems you are telling the truth. My warriors tell me that you have been traveling alone for days, and you were visited last night by a trader. A trader known

to you as Kookerman. True?" the
Bhazz asked.

Somehow I felt that it was hoping
for a lie, so it could justify
killing me. Even allowing me to
swim was only allowing me the
chance to escape, so that it could
justify killing me. I knew now
that it definitely was ordered to
bring me in alive, and only by me
breaking their weird code could it
justify killing me. While it was
keeping me alive right now,
somehow it was not making me feel
very secure for my future.

For as heartless as the Bhazz was,
she was nothing in comparison to
her Singer-Mother.

The Bhazz twittered to its aide,
and the aide chittered to the
warriors, and silently we were
underway.

I wondered what had happened to
Nyzerbad. It was obvious that they
had been searching for him, and I

The Windwalkers Of Xambic

hoped that they were only mildly
interested in me.

But I knew better.

A WINDWALKER

It had taken me four days to get
away from the Farthing, and it
only took us two days of forced
marching to come into sight of the
great Mhyn. As much as I disliked
the company of the spiders, it was
hard not to admire their ability
to march without rest or food. And
I would have been able to admire
them a lot more if they had
bothered to feed me.

"For a weak, runty man-thing, you
show a spark of being worth small
respect. You have not lied to me,
and you have marched without
mewling like so many others we
have captured. I am pleased that I
did not bury a sneem in your
hide." the Bhazz told me as we
came in sight of the 666 web.

"Spidey's got the Big-Tink
Noleaf." I heard being whispered,

178

as we approached the swamp surrounding the Singer camp.

The Grodatts followed us at a respectful distance.

The air was filed with a loud buzzing, and whirring, and it came from the direction of the Grodatts. Soon the source of the buzzing became apparent, as the air was filled with flying, fist-sized, rocks. The Khrx ignored the deadly missiles.

"Seems the Grodatts have regard for you. It's rare for them to unleash their slings." the Bhazz told me, in a manner that I could clearly see was of genuine respect.

"I thought they never argued, never mind getting involved with any type of violence," I replied.

"To the best of our studies they are totally passive, yet even a morabat will fight when cornered. But right now the Grodatts are not cornered, and they are obviously hostile, and before we make the safety of the swamp they will have killed several of my warriors. It seems the Mother-Singers had better re-evaluate these pesky little growers. But, that is not the business for the likes of us -- little man. We of the sneem, are not to concern ourselves. Our job is to obey and execute our orders ... Is that not right?" my proud capturer said with just a touch of what I detected as anger at our superiors. "Soon we will see the depth of your strength -- little man of the sneem."

"And you will enjoy watching?" I asked politely.

The green eye-band flashed over with red, then was green, and unfathomable again, but just for a second I had read this proud warrior.

Four of the Khrx had taken direct hits on their large green eyes and

were left where they died, only
their spear was taken by an
unfeeling comrade-at-arms. While I
wasn't thrilled about my present
situation. I had discovered a real
weakness in the Singers war
structure.

Never once had the highly
intelligent Bhazz communicated
directly with a Khrx, always the
proud Bhazz had twittered to the
little spear-carrier.

Then the aide had chittered to the
Khrx.

Suddenly a large, sharp missile
hit the Bhazz squarely in the
green eye-band. Nothing! The
projectile should have killed the
leader outright, and at the very
least, destroyed its odd chitinous
green sight appendage. But nothing
had happened. What I did notice
was that four of the warriors had
immediately encircled the smaller
aide the moment the rock attack
started. And I noticed that on

several occasions the warriors would take a direct hit before allowing the deadly rocks to hit the smaller aide. I knew that the leader had never condescended to speak directly to any of the mindless warriors.

It would be very important information to find out if the leader was merely too proud to communicate without the go-between, or if the leader was in fact not able to make its orders known to the warriors without the aide.

"I can't help but notice that your warriors take a selfless interest in protecting your spear carrier."

"Yes... It is our way."

"Why is that?" I asked, trying to sound as if I wasn't really that interested, but just mildly curious.

"Questions of this nature will leave you to ripen in the pit.

Beware of such interests in the presence of the Mothers."

"I meant no harm. I, just noticed that one of the Khrx took a fatal blow that was intended for your aide."

"We call the little ones Bha-at, and they are not warriors, so they represent no threat to you. Neither they nor the Kha who tend the Mothers are able to even defend themselves. And because of this we defend them. This little Bha-at that attends me is my friend, and if my warriors were to allow harm to come to such a defenseless member of our race, they would die a very painful death. And if another race were to kill either a Bha-at or a Kha, we warriors would react as you humans would to the senseless slaughter of your children."

"Truly. I meant no disrespect."

"I believe you meant none, for if I did you would spill your life juices into this filthy bog."

"I thought Singers loved bogs."

"We detest anything slimy, but the Sandshrieks will not come into it, and for that reason we are forced to live in it."

I knew that the Singers feared the Sandshrieks, and was trying to phrase a question that the Bhazz would not recognize as an information-gathering-question.

"No more questions. You ask far too many leading questions for a humble trader. Questions that make me wonder what you really are, and your deportment is more in order of a Bhazz than any I have ever encountered before."

"Thank you." I said, realizing the compliment.

"Don't thank me too soon little man. For I think you are too dangerous to live. But, it was my

order to bring you in alive, and
while I see no sense in taking a
dangerous warrior into our camp,
it is not my place to challenge
the ways of the Mothers. So--
While you have been pumping me ...
And you have. I have been forced
to wonder why?"

I shuddered.

I could see no escape from this
creature, and I knew I was no
match for it. I doubted very much
that even a Nhark would best this
creature in single combat.

Soon I was to see.

The camp lay directly in the
center of the fetid swamp, safe
from prying eyes, Sandshrieks, and
flying missiles. Grunts had dug a
deep pit, and from it came the
grunting of fat piggots, and the
high pitched squeal of long eared
morabats. The Khrx grappled me,
and were in the process of hurling
me into the pit, when a twittering
came from the 666 Tetrahedron.

Immediately, a Bha-at approached the Khrx that were about to cast me into the putrid pit. A high angry chittering came from the Bha-at, and a great deal of arm waving and gesturing.

"You get a reprieve from the food pit." came a twittering, but understandable melody from the Bha-at.

"You speak Federation?"

"Obviously I do." came the clear bell-like twitter.

"How come you never spoke on the journey?" I asked.

"Because I have been on none. You were brought in by the Bhazz and her Bha-at. I am the Bha-at of the six Mothers. My charming brother speaks many tongues, but Federation is not one of them. Only the Bhazz and I speak Federation."

The Windwalkers Of Xambic

"What of the Mothers Singers? One of them spoke to me in the village." I challenged.

"Yes, of course the Mothers speak all thoughts. The Mother that spoke to you is still angry with having to communicate with one as baseborn as you. She is for eating you herself, but the other Mothers and I are more interested in what is in your bony head than what is on your little bones. Later, they will strip the meat from your bones. Have patience."

I noticed that the Khrx were weaving a vile green cage. Their four miniature eating-arms were busy extracting a foul viscous substance from their evil tuskor laden mouths. They quickly spun this mess into a sticky rope-like-cage, and they wove this cage around me! Even as I struggled against the sticky mess, I could feel it hardening.

Within minutes it was a hard, but still tacky rope that they suspended over the deep pit.

"Thank the Mothers for their consideration in not dropping me into that vile pit." I told the Bha-at.

"The Mothers have been told that you could escape the pit. This I can't believe, but our Bhazz has respect for you, and even the angry Mother will not defy our Bhazz. For she is very great in our land.It is said she is of the same hatching as our leader."

"The Bhazz are your leaders? I thought the Mothers were in command." I said, looking down into the smelly pit.

"Yes, we lead you to believe this, but as you will never leave the cage alive. I can tell you that while we pamper every whim of the Mothers, they are not our leaders. This camp is my camp, and my brother Bha-at would be second in

command if he had not long been
dominated by his Bhazz. But such
is the way of lust, and his mind
is weak because of being confused
by it."

"You are right, we of the
Federation know less than nothing
of the Singer ways. For on this
short time I can see all our
information about your social
order is wrong."

"Yes, the Bhazz has already told
me of your thirst for knowing our
ways. This thirst will drink you
to death little man. It's a pity."

"It's a pity?" I asked, not
believing my ears.

"Yes, I could use an aide to talk
with about the universe. Only war-
minded Bhazz and my brother Bha-at
have intelligence."

"What of the Mothers?" I asked
innocently.

"What of the Mothers? They have no interest beyond building an empire of trade webs... And glutting on living flesh."

"And you don't share these views... And desires?"

"You are truly a spy! Fortunately, what you learn will only end in the gluttonous belly of a Mother."

"And not yours?" I asked.

"We, the Bha-at eat only vegetables. To us Bha-at, you Federator pigs-- are savage. Though we be caught by ties stronger than intelligence, we putrify ourselves-- never! Think again before you paint us all with your small brush," the small companion of the Bhazz said in anger.

"Ohoo ... A morality," I chuckled.

"A morality that even the Federation falls far short of. But, we are part of a breeding cycle that dictates our ways."

The Windwalkers Of Xambic

"What about cloning your way out of your dilemma?" I asked, innocently enough.

"Can it be you are intellectually interested? Or is it that your curiosity is for spying only?" asked the Bha-at, it's green eye-band glowing brightly.

"A little of both I suppose." I answered truthfully.

"You are a strange creature, Federator. Honest and deceitful--all in one breath. Were it my choice, you would be shipped to the planet Kha immediately."

"Your planet is named after your breeding males?"

"Hardly. Even our stupid Mothersingers wouldn't sing a song of such foolishness. No, the Kha derive their name from the fact that Kha is the only word they ever are able to say. Our breeding males have little in what you Federators call gray-matter. And it seems with each generation they become stupider. Fortunately, almost all the eggs laid, are Kha eggs."

"Why is this?" I asked, my interest blotting out my horrible circumstances.

"Well, if they had enough intelligence to overcome their sexual cravings, they would flee the presence of a Mother, for above all things, a Kha is the most delectable to a Mother."

"You mean desirable." I corrected.

"I know the meanings of Federation words, and I mean delectable in every sense of the word."

"Then, how come your population keeps rising?"

"Never let it be said that the Kha is anything, if not arduous." and after his uttering this, I could almost detect laughter in the twittering of the lonesome Bha-at.

The Windwalkers Of Xambic

"If not for this ghastly cage, this conversation would be stimulating." I said.

The male, that did not lust, looked at me verv closely to see if I was serious, then the strange creature left me to the snarling of the beasts in the pit far below.

For two weeks I remained in the net-cage without food, with only enough water to keep me alive. And in that two weeks the only thing I learned about the Singers was their incredible appetite for eating their horny little mates. And for the persistency of the Kha to mount the ghastly Singers. If nothing else could be said about these loathsome creatures, it could be said that they really proved the ancient axiom about beauty being in the eye of the beholder.

On the fifteenth day they deprived me of water.

By nightfall I was unable to stand
in the cage, and the following day
I slipped in and out of
consciousness. I knew they meant
to weaken my resistance before
questioning me, but, I would have
the last laugh, even if I wouldn't
be around to enjoy the savoring of
it.

Through gummy eyes I watched the
sun go down, and with the moons--
came great white billowy clouds
that diffused the light. Soon the
sky was a great boiling cauldron
of angry, gray-black clouds,
roiling and boiling across the
sky. With the clouds came a cool,
misty rain. Delirious, and on the
threshold of death, I lay on my
back, trying to trap life-giving
water.

The cool mist was soon a cold-
biting-torrent that filled my eyes
and penetrated my body, like a
thinking, life-giving force, that

was determined to drive life into my parched and dying body.

The already slimy, fetid swamp became a river of mud. The deep pit below me filled quickly and its four legged prisoners fled in fear with a squealing and a grunting of mixed fear and pleasure. I wondered if my spittle cage would melt at its base and cause my cage to collapse into the water-filled pit.

I became vaguely aware of falling, then deep, freezing cold. I struggled as my cage became a ropy sack that weighed me down into the deep cold water below. Water filled my mouth, and I tried to hold my breath, but gagged, and a swirling nausea soon overtook me. Then vertigo. Vertigo that ended in blackness. My thoughts were of escape and nothing else-- then I struggled into darkness.

I felt hands on my body. Many small hands. Hands, not chitinous claws! Real hands! I had vague feelings of being rolled over and over.

"He's alive!" came a clear, bell-like voice from out of a gray tunnel. Then I felt myself belching water through my mouth and

I opened my eyes.

Overhead the skies boiled furiously, and from a great frothy crest came a thundering, "Windstriker Ho!" And this rolling thunder came from a giant. A giant riding a massive surfboard on the leading curl of the whirling blackness.

"Stormrider HO!" came a body-rending thunder from not fifty feet away. And it came from a Norse giant that was as tall as the cocata trees that it effortlessly ripped out by the roots. The Norse giant gleefully smashed a storage building to

smithereens with a tree in each
massive fist.

I knew I must be hallucinating.
But I knew I wasn't.

"Is this the one?" came a
reverberating thunder from the
lips of the giant, his great
golden ponytail waving from side
to side as he bent over to peer at
me. I hoped he didn't thunder in
my face, for I knew if he did, my
hearing would be impaired. But he
just grinned a great friendly
flat-toothed grin. He scooped up
both the Grodatts. They had been
holding my head above the swirling
water.

All around the giant -- small
waterspouts formed, whirling and
collapsing with the occasional
spout suddenly spiraling up into
the heavens. The water was now
about two feet deep and rising,
turning the swamp into a lake.

His great hand encircled me ever
so gently, and he sat me on his

shoulder beside the two grinning Grodatts.

"What do you think of Windstriker?" Dilbo said.

For it was Dilbo and Mildleaf that had come to my rescue.

"Pretty impressive," I said, "Hope he doesn't decide to talk to us."

The great ruddy face turned slowly, and I looked into a face alive with amusement. The fathomless blue orbs twinkled like far off stars, and as I gazed into them I felt a temporary vertigo. Not a word was spoken, but my unasked questions were answered.

We three held onto the great, golden braid as the gentle but unpredictable Windstriker headed out of the swamp.

We held tightly to his braid.

Overhead, the mighty Stormrider rode the crest. And on closer observation it could be felt that he guided the direction of the now--full-blown-gale. Around the swamp a great cloud about ten miles in diameter swirled, with its tapered cone-like base boiling in the swamp. The swamp had become a lake of fury.

Reaching higher ground, Windstriker dropped to his knees, then bent forward, allowing us to jump to dry ground.

Overhead, Stormrider was riding the outer edge of the now perfectly circular stormspout. Sheet lightning filled the skies, and an occasional blast of forked lightning would rend a building of the Singers. Every blast of forked lightning was followed by the now familiar "HO" of the surfer above.

With what seemed to me, very accurately controlled strikes.

As Windstriker returned to the swamp, it became almost impossible to see into, for the air was now a living-spout of debris and muddy

water. In the center of the swamp,
only the 666 web of the Singers
remained intact, as if in the eye
of a tornado, or as I suspected,
in another dimension. Whatever
dimension it presently enjoyed was
to soon come to a violent end, as
constant blasts of forked
lightning struck only the web.

Now, I could see that Windstriker
had selected a massive tree, and
he was bearing down on the web
with great speed.

As Windstriker approached the
Tetrahedron, the web turned red-
blue-white, then, the web and
Singers were gone.

Windstriker's club crashed into
the raised base where the
Glimmering web had sat only
seconds before.

No Singers. No camp. And only the
odd Khrx could be seen following
her cohorts into the dunes.

The Windwalkers Of Xambic

The tapered base of the stormspout drew up into the sky.

"HO Stormrider!"

"Ho Windstriker!" came the thundering from above, and the roiling cloud formation rolled out to sea. On its leading curl the two giants rode the curl of white that was now forming.

"It is a strange creature that can command the obedience of the elements." I said to Dilbo.

"Strange is not the unusual on Freefall. Have you not learned this by now?" came Dilbo's simple reply.

"Strange is not the exception in the Universe." I replied.

WINNIE MINNIPLANT

"Now, we had better get you to the Farthing," Dilbo said, putting his arm around my waist. Mildleaf did the same from the other side. And we hobbled to the village.

A solemn procession of Grodatts seemed to materialize from nowhere. Each Grodatt coming forward to touch me. With each touch I felt more like I again belonged to myself, and not the hated Singers. It was as if each touch reaffirmed who I was to the Grodatts—and to me.

"What does all this touching mean?" I asked Dilbo.

"Oh, it is just our way of reassuring you that you are one with the Farthing-- and that you are one with yourself."

"And that's all?"

"No, it's also our way of being sure of who you really are."

"And who am I really-are?"

"Why-- you really are you," Dilbo said innocently. "But, before you take this personal, let me tell you that any Grodatt that left the Farthing for a week, would be greeted in exactly the same manner."

"Sounds paranoid to me."

"Better a little paranoia, than taking a doppleganger into our trust. We have no doubts about you, but ..."

"But what?" I asked.

"But nothing-- we just don't like surprises."

As we approached Mhyn, Winnie came to greet us, and in front of her marched a comalong, its long trunk snuffling the ground ahead as they approached. Suddenly, the comalong ran ahead of Winnie. It ran around

me, snorting and touching me,
snorting louder with each touch.

"It would seem that you have just
passed the acid test, welcome back
to our life." Winnie said in a
small voice, even for her.

She then reached out and touched
me. Just a feather touch, but the
reaction from the circled Grodatts
was incredible. A hooting and
hollering from the adults, little
children turned cartwheels. Then
the circle tightened into a ring
of touching, hugging, loving
beings, and I felt more at one
with myself than I had ever felt
before. Not even when I walked
with the RhaEve had I felt so
complete and at peace with myself.

I had always felt stronger for
being a single, self-reliant
entity, but in the center of that
ring I felt a peace and
tranquility and... Strength, from
being part of a larger life force.
I did not feel fractured and

weaker for only being a segment, and not being the whole entity. For just a moment I felt I was as strong as the circle.

"Come." Winnie said, taking me by a finger. "For while the ghlaming has rebonded your mind. You are still in need."

Winnie's tiny fingers encircled only one finger, yet it was enough support that both Mildleaf and Dilbo were able to release their grip on me and on wobbly legs I followed Winnie to the small oval door in the Mhyn.

"First we must clean up your body, then we can see what can be done about healing." Winnie said, smiling up to me.

"Healing? You mean feeding. I'm not sick, just starved."

"There are many ways to be sick, Marples... You don't mind if I call you Marples do you?" Winnie asked, blushing, at the sight of my nakedness. I set about scrubbing myself with a large pink seasponge.

"You are clean enough. Now into the ghlam with you." Winnie said, leading me to the steaming tub that could easily accommodate twenty bodies. The pool was perfectly round with three step-seats that completely encircled the small pool.

"If it wasn't for these steps, a person could swim in this oversized bathtub." I said to Winnie.

"Oh my! What a thing to say about a ghlam pool." Winnie said from the other room. I had spoken very quietly, yet Winnie had heard me. I thought this strange. So I whispered into my hand that I was hungry, just loud enough for my fingers to hear.

"I'm fixing some nourishment. Don't be impatient." came the

clear bell-like tinkle of her dainty-- and amused voice.

"How do you do that?" I asked.

"Do what?" Winnie said, coming into the now heavily misted bathing room.

"You know what. It was impossible for you to hear me, yet you did. How?" I asked Winnie.

"All things will eventually become known. Have patience my little friend." came a soft melodious voice from the now-dense pink mist that filled the room, making it impossible to see more than a few feet clearly.

"Little friend?" I thought to myself.

And I thought of many things as the now dense pinkness made it impossible to see even my own fingers clearly. I thought of my lifetime friend that had crashed into the sea, trapped in her metal coffin. For some reason I thought

of her as being more than a
suitcase of crystals.

I thought of her as a woman. A
woman of living warmth. I felt her
presence in the pool. I felt her
great liquid eyes upon me ... with
love. I felt her caress me. I felt
the very essence of her.

"Where am I?" I asked a hazy
shape.

"You are in the Ghlaming pool."
came a musical voice from the
other side of the pool.

"Who are you?" I asked.

"I am many things. I am all
things, and I am nothing."

"Are you real?" I asked, already
knowing the answer.

"I'm as real as real can be."

"Are you real in a sense that I
could understand."

"Yes. I am that real."

The Windwalkers Of Xambic

"Are you a living, breathing, person?"

"Yes I am all of that. And I am much much more than any of that, but for now you should sleep."

"I will drown if I fall asleep in this pool."

"Trust me. You will never drown in this pool."

Somehow I knew that TC was in the pool with me. Somehow I felt that TC was part of the strange-warm-personal body of the pool. Somehow I knew that I was safe, as I had always been in her capable caring hands... Hands? I thought as I drifted...

Rise and shine Marples Tinkerman. I know you are awake. Open those big brown eyes and face the world." said a familiar voice, yet it was a voice that I could never remember having heard before.

"Why you're Winnie!" I said, opening my eyes.

"She sure is." laughed Dilbo from the other side of the small bed I was in.

"How long?" I asked.

"Long enough. You look strong enough to wrestle a piggot in a mud patch." Dilbo said, grinning.

"Don't much desire to wrestle a piggot. But I do feel great. I have a thousand questions." I said to Winnie.

"Yes I imagine you do, but for the present I am going to leave the room while you get dressed."

"I had the strangest dream in that hot tub." I told Dilbo as I put on the clothing supplied for me. It was a one-piece cassock, complete with oversize hood, and it, was the color of sand. "Good camouflage if a person was on the run." I said to Dilbo.

Dilbo felt the fabric.

"My father had several identical to it. Mother made them for him. Is there a great-cloak to go with Tink's cassock?" Dilbo asked quietly.

"Yes it's in here by the table. Come and eat. You must be hungry Dilbo. For I know the last two weeks have been hard on you." came the bell-like tone of Winnie's happy voice.

"What about me? Don't you think I'm hungry?" I asked.

"How could you be hungry? You've just spent two weeks in the Ghlaming-pool. You could live on your ghlam-energy for a month and still be healthy. But I suppose you think you're hungry. You silly little boys always think you're hungry."

"Silly little boys!" we challenged, together. Winnie only laughed.

Sitting at the table and enjoying the delicious melon my good feelings soured as I looked out through the wall at the scene below.

FARTHING IN THRALL

"What the hell is going on?" I asked Dilbo.

"While you were recuperating in the ghlam, the Singers came back in force. Great force! They have moved onto a great white outcropping of quartz."

"How far away?" I asked.

"About a click." Dilbo replied.

"Well that's better than having the filth right in front of your village," I said, putting the melon down.

"Something wrong with the melon?" Winnie asked.

"You know what's wrong with the melon. Whats more, I think you know what's wrong with everything. The thing that I don't know is why you don't do something about it," I said, bitterly.

"Don't talk to Mom like that!"
Dilbo said, all but coming across
the table in a sudden defensive
anger completely alien to a
Grodatt's make-up.

"Oho! So you little guys got
feelins after all."

"Sure we do ...But we are not
savages, and we work very hard at
being civilized with each other."

"Winnie—I apologize for whatever
Dilbo thought I meant, but I don't
apologize for what I meant, as it
was not an insult."

"What was it then?" challenged
Dilbo, still miffed.

"I was just curious why Winnie
hasn't sent these varmints back to
wherever they come from. Obviously
they are an unwanted and dangerous
group of trespassers. So why not
send them from whence they came.
Why not?" I said with a smile.

"Aghhh... Don't show all those
carnivorous teeth!" Dilbo said--

214

Shaking his head like a little child saying no to medicine.

"Carnivorous? I'm not carnivorous, now that's an insult... Open. Pure, and direct. And don't change the subject. We were talking about why your mother doesn't send these pests packing."

"Wish I could. They would have long been history, as would all the other off world pests, but I have not that kind of power." Winnie said.

"Do you deny that you have powers?" I challenged.

"Powers as you think of them ...I have none." Winnie answered, in a manner that made me believe her... Yet!

"Then you have access to them!" I said, not letting go

"Not in the sense you mean Tink, but I do have an ear that will sometimes listen."

"And if you ask-- and if this ear listens-- could the dirty spiders be sent packing?"

"You think I don't ask?" Winnie said with tears in her eyes.

"Proud of yourself." Dilbo said, getting up to follow his mother. Me too! And soon we were all standing in a circle, as is normal for Grodatts – Hugging...

"You had better be careful or you will become human," Winnie chided me.

"Hey! I'm the human. You two are the Grodatts."

"Wrong right across the board as usual." laughed Dilbo.

"To tell you the truth Tink, we have often wondered what kind of a Federation you're from, if you are the best trouble shooter."

"Haaay. That's nasty," I complained, and we all laughed. And I knew then was not the time to continue probing as to why Winnie didn't take a physical stand against the Singers.

"One last question. Then no more." I promised.

"Ask, but I don't guarantee that I will be able to answer."

"Did you bring the Windwalkers to save me?"

"No ...I didn't bring them." Winnie said quickly. Too damn quickly to suit me.

"Let me rephrase that question." I said.

"You said one question." Dilbo said strongly.

"Tink is right. My answer was evasive. Tink I know that you believe I have powers that I don't have, but that is only because you don't understand any of us who really belong here."

"Help me to understand."

"We are trying, but it is not as simple as you may believe it to be. You come from a system that deals with facts and figures that will respond to a given stimulus. Here on The One Branch, that has never been the case. But I did plead your unique case, and my pleas fell on ears that would listen. This time we were fortunate and you live because of a whim. Next time we may not be so lucky." Winnie said with sadness and feeling.

"Who did you plead to?" I asked.

"You have been given an honest answer to your question. And that's the end of questioning. For you are too close to that which is better left untalked about," Dilbo said, with finality.

I was so close to solving the riddle of this wacky planet, and I was so damn far away...

The Windwalkers Of Xambic

Why would these honest little people not talk openly? Who had Winnie made her plea to?

Was TC somehow still functional? Or had the dream in the pink room-of-mists been merely a dream?

We three sat in the safety of Mhyn. Yet the Farthing below was in thrall. A dozen Khrx camped at the one door leading in and out of the Mhyn. And every Grodatt below was accompanied by a Grunt. Not a Grodatt moved a foot from their tiny housey-- without the presence of a Grunt.

And none were allowed the chance of escaping into the desert or into the greater safety of the Mhyn.

CROP FAILURE

"Is it my imagination, or is the fwa-foo failing?" I asked.

"Good observation Tink. Soon the non-growers will see what they are about to reap." Dilbo said, with a wide grin.

"What are they doing wrong?" I asked.

"Nothing... Not a darn thing."

"Then why are the gardens not growing?"

"Have you ever heard of emathy-related plants?" Dilbo asked.

"Empathy related?"

"No, not Empathy--Emathy. I suppose the closet that you Federated growers get to emathy is giving your plants a lot of tender-loving-care. At least that's what the Digabouts call it.

The Windwalkers Of Xambic

They claim a good gardener must employ a lot of TLC if that gardener expects good results."

"And you Grodatts use?"

"It's not what we use. It's what the Digabouts call having a green thumb." Dilbo said.

"Sure, but having a green thumb is just paying attention to the plant's needs. Proper humidity, keeping the NPK on the money, exact photoperiods, micro and macro nutrients, things like that are easy to learn. Surely you don't expect me to believe that there is anything supernatural about growing a weed?"

"Nobody expects you to believe anything Tink. But in the last two weeks the fwa-foo has quit growing," Dilbo said.

"Completely?" I asked.

"Oh yes! Very completely," came the musical voice of Winnie.

"And the Grodatts are not sabotaging the plants?" I asked.

"Shame on you for thinking that a grower could ever consider such an uncivilized act. No, the plants will not grow for anyone other than a Grodatt-- or a Twigg," Winnie said, with conviction.

"Will other plants grow for off-worlders?" I asked, looking down to the dying patch below. Not a Grodatt was allowed into his own patch, only the Grunts watered and tended the plants.

"Everything-- but fwa-foo." Dilbo replied.

"You know that on their own planet the Grunts are considered to be master-growers." I told Dilbo.

"Well that may be. But here on The One Branch only the Twiggs and the Grodatts are able to grow the lesser peep-weed," Winnie said, with conviction.

The Windwalkers Of Xambic

"That means that the crop will fail and that the Singers will be forced to take harsh actions. Doesn't that bother you?"

"No reason to be concerned about a temporary situation. Long after all you off-worlders are no more. The One Branch will be again in harmony. And we-- the twigs of the branch will be once more in safety on the boughs of the Tree." Winnie said with a strange light in her eye...

GRODATTS FLEE FARTHING

The Grodatts were herded daily to
their little gardens where they
were forced to sit on the wall
while the Grunts tended their
patches. The plants continued to
die.

Then without warning the Grodatts
were gone.

The Grunts continued to dig and
tend to the now dead gardens and
the Khrx patrolled in front of the
Mhyn-Gate with an evil vengeance,
their very presence an angry
threat.

After the Grodatts had been gone
for ten clicks we were visited by
two Bha-at and a Bhazz of such
bearing that comes only with the
wielding of great power.

The Windwalkers Of Xambic

"Marples Tinkerman, the Bhazz of all the Singers, Khriii the Noble will give you your freedom," came a strong calling from one of the identical Bha-at.

"My freedom is guaranteed by the rights given to the humblest of Federated subjects. Never have I doubted my freedom but if your Bhazz has other thoughts that trouble her, possibly I could be of some help in her plight" I said, with a wide grin, showing all of my teeth. As these were not Grodatts and I wished them to see the teeth of a free Federator.

"If you are free-- prove it." came the crisp reply.

"Only a fool would strive to prove that which is obvious."

"Beware or you will never leave the face of this strange ball of water," came the twittering.

"Then we will grow old together on this planet. Are you not the Bha-at that threatened me with my death in the swamp?"

"I was the voice of the Mothers in the swamp, and we did talk. But I truly never threatened you. And if I would have obeyed the wishes of the Mothers then-- You would not be here now to dispute so cleverly for these little growers."

"Having a little trouble with the weed?" I laughed.

"You know as well as I that we are on this forlorn ball of water for only one purpose. We mean these little growers no harm and have never harmed them but we must have them return to grow the weed." came the twittering with what I could tell was an urgency to strike an arrangement.

"But if I am a lowly prisoner what possible good can I be to such an august and all powerful group such as you represent?"

The Windwalkers Of Xambic

"You are clever Marples and we know of your past talents at solving problems considered unsolvable. I am empowered to give you your freedom and you may travel unhindered and unmolested by our very large and powerful army that presently controls this planet. We have the power and means to keep you in that fortress forever. But our intentions are peaceful. We only seek the weed. Talk to the Grodatts for us."

"Wny should I sell these honorable little people out to your version of freedom when they have their freedom now—without any strings attached. Give me one logical reason that could benefit them," I told the silent group.

"We would leave this planet if we had the means of growing the weed on our own planet. Is that not a good reason?'

"When the Federation is apprised of your unwanted presence you will leave." I told the Bha-at quietly.

The Bha-at twittered to the other Bha-at and he in turn twittered to the haughty Bhazz. "I notice that your leader bares no arms. Now I give you your freedom to live for I am armed and could destroy the three of you long before your stupid Khrx could intervene. I believe I owe you my life. And I will now give you yours in return. Go before I change my mind."

"So... You are The Tinkerman. We have not been able to read you. But we believe you to be-- he who tinkers. And it is because of this that you were spared in the swamp, and because of this I know you are not capable of killing an unarmed group-- even this group who you dislike so strongly," twittered the Bha-at. He turned and twittered to the other Bha-at and

it in turn twittered to the leader
known as-- Kriii the Noble Bhazz.

"You people had better get your
communications in order if you
plan to take on the Federation."

"We have no concern for the
Federation. They need our instant
tetrahedrons of shipping. Every
day that our webs don't function
causes great discomfort for your
busy Federation. Even now
medication is not being
transported to outpost stars at
the rim of the Galaxy. We may be
losing financial gain but your
Federation is the real loser.
No...Your precious Federation will
not attack us, nor will they harm
us in any way."

"I admit what you say about the
Federation makes sense, and you
are right about me. To attack your
unarmed party would be cold-
blooded murder and the thought of
it is so repugnant to me that even
thinking of it makes me ill. But

you have the Nhark and Nyzan
empires to contend with. And they
have no compunction of going to
war-- or even cold-blooded murder
for that matter."

"True. Let me plead this logic to
the Bhazz."

A high pitched twittering and
angry waving of arms took place,
that would have been comical if
not for the anger flowing between
the two Bha-at. Finally, the Bhazz
held both of her long arms above
her head. Truly she was not of the
warring class of Bhazz, her arms
were almost without tendons and
her claws had grown and turned in
upon themselves making her unable
to even feed herself, never-mind
carry a war javelin. She stepped
closer to me. Her lips opened in a
grotesque smile for her mouth was
toothless. Only her weak-yellow
eyes displayed any strength.

"You have truth about you
Tinkerer. I will leave the Bha-at

with you. He believes in your fairness. We have over a hundred thick headed Mothers and fifty thousand Khrx on this planet. And all of them wish you dead. I will stay them for as long as I can came a dry rasping from a voice-box long unused.

"I thank you Noble Khriii for your understanding," I said awe-struck that a Khriii of the Singers would ever stoop to communicating directly with any being other than her personal Bha-at.

The war party had been held at a distance by their Bhazz. On an order from their Bha-at they quickly brought a webbed, stick-like contrivance for carrying their leader away.

Then they were gone. Only the Bha-at remained.

"It seems we are stuck with each other." twittered the Bha-at with definite humor in his tinkling voice.

231

"Do you have a name?" I asked the Bha-at.

"Only Khriii, the Leader has a name."

"Well if we are to travel together you must have a name. What do you think would be a fitting name Dilbo?" I asked the approaching Grodatt.

"How about Tinkle."

"Tinkle?"

"Sure. He tinkles when he talks."

"How do you feel about being called Tinkle?" I asked the silent Bha-at.

"I have never considered having a name. But if it will help in our joint endeavor... Why yes. I like the name. It sounds much like your own name... Tink--erman... Tink--le. Yes, I would be honored to have such a name. On Kha the name Marples Tinkerman has long stood for valor and fairness. Yes I

232

would be deeply honored to bear such a name. I will try to deserve it."

"And I am Dilbo Minniplant. Today will be a day long remembered in the Farthing."

"On Kha too. Never has the Noble Khriii stooped to vocal transfer of thoughts."

We walked to Dilbo's little peep-patch.

"Could you not teach the Grunts to grow the weed, then our problems could be solved without bloodshed." asked the Bha-at.

"I could bring my own garden back to life with just one clone as a start. But that is all I could do."

"Surely it would be easy to supervise the growing of another garden, or of many gardens if you had willing capable helpers."

"Growing the weed of peep is not like growing any other plant. Each patch will only respond to the one grower." Dilbo said bending over and feeling the soil. "They have done much damage already. It would take patience to coax even this patch back to life. It is not dead, but it is very close."

"Then you must stay and do it. Marples and I can look for the villagers. We must do something before the Singers have their way," Tinkle said with genuine concern.

"Why are you concerned with the fate of Grodatt's?" I asked.

"Why are you?" the Bha-at replied with a buzz. "Do you think because you are a human that you have deeper better motivated feelings then all others?"

"Tinkle is right Marples. You should both at least try and see if there is a solution before the

Khrx run amok and murder all living creatures on the Branch."

"That would bring about the end of Kha." I said to Dilbo.

"By the federation?" asked Tinkle.

"You know better than that." I replied.

"Then you know of the greater problem?" asked Tinkle.

"We all do. Certainly the peep-weed is a small thorn to both the Federation and to your Singers, but that is of very small import in comparison to the greater picture that could be played because of what is happening here," I replied, looking deep into the eye-band of the Bha-at...But I had not enough information to read the Bha-at.

"What you and I accomplish, or fail to, will make the difference of Bha-at at eventually coming into the federation as a valid

member of a greater society."
Tinkle said.

"Or becoming extinct!" I
challenged

"Yes... Or becoming extinct."
Tinkle replied without a trace of
a tinkle in his normally musical
voice.

We set out in search of the
Grodatts.

Mostly we hoped to find Nhioby and
Nyzerbad before...

DIGABOUTS AID GRODATTS

As Tinkle and I struck out in search of the Grodatts, we knew that the fate of a great many lives rested with our being successful in our mission.

"What if we are not able to convince the growers to teach us of Kha the secrets of the weed?" Tinkle asked, returning the salute to a group of heavily armed Khrx.

"Then your warriors will commit a crime against these innocents."

"Will this precipitate a war?"

"No. but it will cause severe reprimands against your people," I said.

"Then we must not fail. Look, the host is coming."

"I thought we were to travel without interference."

"Interference?"

"What would you call it, if not interference?"

"I'd call it respect-- Deep respect. Look! They salute you."

"Why would they salute me? I have not done anything to warrant anything yet."

"They show you the respect you deserve my little friend. Never in our history has a Khriii spoken aloud to anyone. For a Khriii to address a non Bha-at is great respect, but to actually directly address a member of another race is unheard of, and is beyond the understanding of a simple Khrx."

"Do you understand her reasoning?"

"Yes and I respect her greatness for putting aside a lifetime of tradition for the greater outcome of our people. She will be a Bhazz to sing of in the darkness. For it will bring light to the hearts of all who can understand the song."

The Windwalkers Of Xambic

"There might be hope for your people after all."

"And there might be hope for your's." Tinkle said, with a tinkle in his already musical voice. This tinkle was one I was learning was--a tinkle of humor.

"Your popularity with the host will only make the Mothers hate you deeper... if possible, for they are for doing some very unpleasant things to you. And to hell with the outcome."

We walked for two clicks into the desert before we were able to look to a dune and not be saluted by a Khrx.

On the third click we had headed north and were setting up camp at seaside when Tinkle put his soft clawless hand on my arm. His chitinous sight-organ turned purple. "I have something to say if we are going to continue together."

"You have a confession?" I laughed.

His sightband turned purple, then returned to its normal dull green-gold. "I have lied to you Marples and I must put it right."

"So, do it if it's bothering you."

"I feel the guilt of carrying this lie for days." Tinkle said and the eye-band flashed purple again.

"We all swerve from the straight and narrow. Actually what is the truth to one man is a lie to another. Could you imagine a poker player being unable to bluff?"

"We of Kha don't play poker. Deviating from what we know to be a fact is a wrong that we are unable to live with."

"What could you have said to make you feel so guilty?"

Again the flash of purple. "I told you that it was below us of the Bha-at to eat meat."

"And this is not entirely true?"

"No. Not entirely. We don't eat our own kind as the Mothers do. And we don't eat any other sentient beings. Fish, crustaceans and shellfish and other unthinking creatures we are guilty of eating."

"Do you feel guilt for eating-- or guilt for misleading me?"

"Both!" Tinkle blurted, his eye-band a bright purple.

"We all carry our crosses, and as crosses go, yours seems pretty light to me."

"You are not upset that I have broken the truth?" Again the bright purple eye-band.

"No. but I will be upset if you don't find some firewood for us to cook supper with... Are you going to eat with me or are you going to punish yourself?" I said laughing.

We traveled for many clicks and I became aware that Tinkle was a highly principled and extremely empathetic creature.

"How can you be the son of a Singer?" I mused as we prepared for sleep.

"Each culture surely had its periods of embarrassment, your earlier culture can hardly be one of pride."

"True. It took us almost ten thousand years to develop a fair and equitable society." I admitted. "We of the Federation know our system is not perfect but we try! How do you justify what is taking place here on Xambic?"

"I have no say in the events that are decreed by the leader. My personal conduct is all I can be responsible for."

"Bull-shit. We are all responsible for the attitude of the culture we are a part of." I said, preparing to lay down in the soft cocata-frond bed I'd just made.

"How do you figure that?" Tinkle said his eye-band silver.

"We are all integral parts of the final sum of our society, and as such we are responsible for it's every mandate."

"All of us?" Tinkle asked from his frond bed.

"Every damn one of us!"

"No cause to be angry with me."

"I'm not angry with you personally Tinkle but in my job I am always confronted with the same problem. And sometimes I get angry at the evil head of collective intolerance."

"Collective intolerance. But how can I be guilty of a system that I can do nothing about?"

"That's the god damn problem!" I said, sitting up.

"What's the god-damn problem?"
Tinkle said getting up, his eye-
band was glowing a bright red.

And so Tinkle and I talked until
sunrise. I learned much about
Tinkle as an individual and he
learned much about Tinkle as an
individual. And more important he
learned that if only one Domino
will elect to push hard against
its fellow Domino. Whatever is—
doesn't have to be...It just takes
one falling Domino to change a
society.

Could Tinkle be that Domino?

Could I help him fall?

With these thoughts in mind we
trudged further east in search of
Nyzerbad and Nhioby. For if we
didn't find them in time... the
Kha Nation would never have the
chance to be Dominoes. They would
simply be wheat to be cut by the
indifferent reaper of fate.

The Windwalkers Of Xambic

And then my mission would be one of failure.

"Stand and deliver!"

"Stand and deliver?" I repeated aloud, not sure I was hearing right.

"Make no fun of us. Stand and deliver. Else we'll run you and the bugman through with cold sneems." came the angry voice.

"Come out so we can better understand why we should be giving up our sneems to nothing more than an angry voice that seems not to be in touch with reality."

"We'll teach the likes of you about reality friend-to-a-bug," came a feminine voice. Not soft and friendly, but shrewish.

From behind rocks and from the living sand itself strange dirty creatures welled up around us. Tinkle moved closer to me, as was his way. Never had he carried a weapon nor needed one when in the

fierce protective presence of a
Bhazz. This would be a traumatic
experience for the unarmed Bha-at
to face an enemy without his
shield of Khrx led by a Bhazz.

"Don't be afraid Tinkle. For an
enemy that is talking is not
usually ready for violence."

"Are you sure?" came Tinkle's
reply.

"Not a bit," I grinned.

Tinkle twittered and his eye-band
£lashed pink for just a second.
But it was enough for me.

"Who's the leader?"

"What's it to you-- you runty
little bugman," came a casual
reply from a thin-as-a-stick male
that had a head the shape and
color of a dirty turnip. A turnip
with a little patch of filthy hair
sticking straight up.

"Can't see any reason to talk to
the back end of a jackass when the

other stupid end is so close." I
replied.

"What's a jack-ass?" came a
challenge from a male about half
as tall as the turnip head but
this one was at least five times
as wide. And looked extremely
powerful. I noticed that he was
much cleaner, even his single
garment, a loincloth was cleaner
than that of the stick man.

"Why a jackass is strong
determined, and has a mind of his
own," I said without telling a
lie.

"Why then we are all jackasses."
came a wispy voice from a young
woman easily weighing over four
hundred pounds.

"Why I believe you are," I said,
looking over the dirt covered mob
in their filthy threadbare
loincloths.

"Think any of us be more of a
jackass than the rest?" came a

sensual lisp from an extremely
lovely girl of about twenty.

"I'm sure that some of you are
greater jack-asses than others but
for now I can't tell who the
greatest jack-ass is."

"Not a bad feller ...   Even if
he be company to a bug," the heavy
set male said with finality.

"Kinda cute for a dwarfy," the
sensual girl lisped.

"Leaving the stranger be till Moma
gets a chance to figure out what
we gonna do with him and the bug,"
came a gentle voice from a tall
grinning male. "Names Mel, these
be my brothers and sisters. Pay
them no nevermind as they be
harmless enough if you don't start
the trouble."

"Who are you?" I asked.

"Why... We be Digabouts. Everybody
knows bout us You must be the
newcomer that be livin with the
Grodatts. Lest you be a Grodatt,"

The Windwalkers Of Xambic

Mel the Digabout said, with a grin.

"No I'm not a Grodatt. But I take no offense at being called a Grodatt."

"You be lookin like a cute little Grodatt to me. Sure enough." the big girl said with a leer.

"Be leavin the stranger be, Kinky. Lotsa other men here at Digabout for you to be pesterin. No call to be flirtin with a prisoner."

"I'm a prisoner?" I asked.

"Till Moma figures what to do with you. Travelin with a bug won't go in your favor, course if you can give Moma a reason why a man be floppin round in the dunes with a bug...." Mel said with his perpetual grin.

"Can't fool Moma." Mel said, and they all agreed.

That night the Digabouts dug roots and Tinkle and I shared the meal

in silence. The following morning
we struck out for the village of
Digaboot. As the sun set on the
flat horizon the two moons gleamed
dully over the village known as
Digaboot. It was a mud thatched
conglomeration of low shed-type
structures. Each shed could easily
house at least fifty people
comfortably and there were
hundreds of these sheds. Digaboot
was a much larger community than I
had envisioned.

Tinkle and I were escorted through
the wet muddy streets to the only
round building in Digaboot. It was
directly in the center of the
village, with all the shed-like
buildings running out from it, not
unlike spokes from the hub of a
wheel.

As we approached the round,
thatched building we were
surrounded by a living wall of
Grodatts. I put my arm around
Tinkle, and could feel his

uncertainty in his frail body. Yet, his eyeband glowed a bright gold as he looked to me.

"Don't fear them. They mean you no harm," I said quietly.

"I am not afraid." came the soft tinkle in reply.

"Good. For these Grodatts may hate your army, but as an individual they bear you no malice," I said.

"I know that, but it is still uncomfortable to be in the camp of what my leaders consider to be the enemy."

"I have spent a lifetime as the outsider, so I know exactly how you feel." I said.

The eye-band flashed purple again.

"What have we here?" a thin white haired woman said, approaching Tinkle and myself.

"I'm Marples Tinkerman and this here is my good friend Tinkle."

"Not very choosy about your friends, are you?" she replied.

"Choosy enough," I replied, getting angry.

"No need for gettin smart with Moma. Wanna fight?" the heavy set Digabout challenged.

"Not right now but hold that thought jackass," I replied.

""Mind your manners Tuffy. The Grodatts say that Marples is a regular kinda fella. So don't be fighting with him."

"Aw Mom I like him well enough," Tuffy said sheepishly.

"Don't pay attention to Tuffy, he just likes a friendly fight now and then. He is my baby and with all his brothers and sisters being older, he has always had to fight."

"Should fight summon else. Summon his own size." Complained Boozy Bentleaf, coming to my aid.

"No problems. Is the whole of the Farthing here?" I asked Boozy.

"All cept for Dilbo and Winnie. And Winnie will never leave the Mhyn so I suppose the whole village is here." Mildleaf the Mouser said, coming forward. Even though I had only know these Grodatts a short time, it felt good to see all their friendly faces in this village of mud.

In the far corner of the round meeting house I spotted an old traveling companion. His great-coat hiding his face from view, but his lack of mud and almost invisible gray cloak told me who he really was.

"Mildleaf. I want you and Boozy to promise me something," I said to the Mouser.

"Ask anything. We be happy ta do it," Mildleaf replied.

"Then take care of Tinkle for me."

"Why can't you take care of Tinkle?" Boozy asked.

"Because I have business that could be dangerous," I said. "Now will you both give me your word?"

"We all will," came a reply from many small voices.

I headed through the throng of over five hundred bodies not letting the gray cloak out of my sight. It too was on the move and in a direction away from me. As I knew it would be.

"You don't understand what happened," Augustus Fung said, stepping out of the throng in front of me. I quickly stepped around him only to be confronted by LeKlunc the Nhark.

"All of you are in on it. Is that it LeKlunc?"

"It wasn't like you thought it to be." LeKlunc said, holding both his hands behind himself. I unsheathed my short stabbing

254

sneem, and from behind his back LeKlunc produced one of equal length. I had seen the berserking of LeKlunc in the swamp and knew how deadly he was, so I stepped in crabwise, and so did LeKlunc. When he was only feet away, I slashed out with my longer sneem. LeKlunc parried, with his also hidden, longer sneem. Meanwhile, Scram the traitor, who had sold me in the desert, was getting away. I tried to bypass LeKlunc but found myself face to face with Augustus Fung.

Augustus had a net whirling in front of me and LeKlunk was closing in from behind me. I darted directly at Fung as he threw his net. I sidestepped and LeKlunc rushed into the net.

I went for the door but hands grabbed from everywhere and I felt my movement being taken from me as I collapsed under the weight of the wall of bodies.

"You will have to quit struggling. Or we will be here all night." came a calm voice from behind me.

"Let me go. What the hell is happening?" I screamed at nobody in particular.

"You must quit struggling. Scram is gone, and you will just be chasing the wind. Scram is talented at being evasive. Let me explain who and what he is and if after I explain why he left you, you are still inclined to hunt him. Then I will help you. But first let me explain..."

"Let me go. Then explain." I challenged.

"No! First I explain, then you will be set free." came the same calm voice.

"Bring the Bha-at. You do trust the Bha-at don't you my little friend or do you suspect the Bha-at too of being deceitful?"

The Windwalkers Of Xambic

"No, I trust the Bha-at. Now let me go." I demanded.

"First you talk to the Bha-at, then I will have my people release you. Now quit struggling."

The crowd moved out of the way as a small procession, headed by the Mouser and Bentleaf approached with a smile on their small brown faces.

"Tell me that Scram the Quick didn't desert me, then this monster that is holding me can release me," I said trying to turn my head around to see my captor.

Not a chance. The human vice held me firmer than a form-a-seat from my days in the photon-drive-warpers.

"Who is this Scram-the-Quick that you are out of control over?" Tinkle twittered his eyeband silver.

"Scram was my traveling partner in the Desert. He tipped off the

Singers where I was and I would have died in the Singers meat pit if I had not been saved by the Windwalkers.

"So! Your incredible stupid anger has been precipitated by a traitor who sold you to die at the hands of the Singers."

"Yes," I said trying to break free.

"And if this first individual that you traveled with had not sold you out to the Mothers, then...?"

"Then I would have no grievance," I admitted.

"Then you have no grievance as the first-- and the second of your traveling companions deserted you for the same reason."

"Which was?" I challenged getting angry at the Bha-at.

"Which was to save your life."

"Bull-malarkie. I know that Kookerman escaped because even he

258

was unable to overcome a host of sixty warriors but that was not treachery. I'm not angry with him as he had no choice."

"Then you should have less grievance with your first companion for while the second one-- the one you falsely name as Kookerman fled to fight another day. The first companion fled so that we would follow him and give you a chance to escape."

"Are you telling me that Scram not only didn't sell me out, but in fact put his own life in jeopardy by leading your warriors away from me?"

"That's what I'm trying to tell you." The eyeband glowed a bright yellow.

"Then how did your troops find me?"

"That was easy. When we lost track of you we simply followed Kookerman until he found you."

"Let me get this straight. While Kookerman was trying to help me, what he was doing was really leading your troops to me?"

"Yes. Kookerman has a strong signal, and we could capture him anytime we wanted to."

"Are you saying that even now the Singers could capture him and his mad woman any time that they want to?" I asked quietly.

"Certainly. We have always known of his every movement. His signal is too strong to shield."

"Then why does he keep hiding from your troops"'

"Probably because he thinks we are stupid enough to believe his lame story about being a brain damaged trader."

"The Singers don't think he is a brain ..."

"Oh we think he is involved with trading and stealing, and we certainly know he has many kinds of brain damage but we also know who he is." Tinkle said his eyeband pink.

"And that is?" I challenged.

"This is not the time for such questions Tink."

"Would you lie to me?" I challenged.

The eyeband went blood red.

"Whisper in my ear." I ordered and Tinkle did.

"Let me go. I am sure that Scram is guilty of nothing but trying to help me."

"And you have no grievance with him?" came the voice.

"None that I know of. Now let me go. The Bha-at has told me of the events of that day. And a Bha-at tells no lies."

"Your word as a commander of the Federation and as-- He who walked with the RhaEve."

"I give my word" I said.

My captor released me and I whirled to strike for I had not promised anything about personal retribution.

It was a woman. A small smiling woman.

"Welcome to Digaboot Commander Tinkerman. I am the mother of this commune of growers."

"The mother?" I asked.

"Yes. Everyone calls me Moma Grime."

"Is there a Papa Grime?" I asked with a grin."

"There could be... Are you applying for the job?"

"If it were not for my responsibility to the Federation I

would sweep you off your lovely feet." I said bowing low.

We both laughed.

The crowd roared with approval and I sheathed my sneems.

"You have already met my charming children. Come, I will arrange for sleeping quarters for your companion and yourself."

Tinkle and I were given quarters with the Grodatts and after two months it became obvious that the Grodatts were unable to grow their crop of fwa-foo in the rich mud of Digaboot.

Kookerman had been reported in the vicinity of the Farthing of Longbottom. I immediately decided to leave for the Farthing, and it was no surprise when the miserable Grodatts decided to return with me to their familiar land of clean sandy soil.

"If you ever decide to come a courting. You will always be

welcome big fella." Moma Grime laughed. The Grodatts cheered.

THE RETURN TO LONGBOTTOM

We left the large valley of terraced gardens and the muddy streets of Digaboot in good spirits, good spirits that were to change very quickly.

"Why could you not grow your fwa-foo on the terraces?" I asked Ican Grodatt.

"Fwa-foo d'n wanta grow." he replied simply.

"You mean you can't make it grow," I corrected the headman of Longbottom.

"No! I say fwa-foo d'n wanta grow. Dats what I be meanin."

"What you are saying is that the seed has a mind of its own and will grow or not grow as it sees fit?" I laughed.

"Too many teeth!" came the flash reply from all the Grodatts that were near enough to see and listen.

"Sorry," I apologized keeping my lips tight.

"Pology cepted. Know yer not an insulter ta me."

And in the next click I learned the secret to growing the peep-weed of Longbottom. And I could see that the Grodatts would have been better named--The Grodatts of fwa-Foo, for non other than a Grodatt could ever grow a Grodatt plant. And non other than a Twigg could grow a Twigg plant. And that was the way of it! So the Grodatts headed home to their personal destiny.

The second day into the desert we became aware of being followed. Our resident comalongs came in out of the desert and formed a perimeter around our small group. The Grodatts seemed unconcerned, but the comalongs kept moving in close and nose touching, as if to make sure that the small people were okay.

This was something I had not noticed before-- the Grodatts here were all adult... where were the children?

"Do you notice anything strange?" I asked Tinkle.

"Everything I notice on this planet is strange," Tinkle replied, his eyeband pink.

"This is not a funny question, how come the old pink-eye?"

"Pink eye? What is pink eye?"

"It's the color your eyes get when you think something is funny. Surely you know," I said grinning.

"I'm that easy to read?"

"As long as you don't wear sunglasses you will be an open book for anyone that can see. Now

about what you think is so funny,"
I asked seriously.

"Well to tell you the truth, I
find my environment and
surroundings as easy to read as
you do my sight appendage."

"Back to the question."

"I'll make a deal."

"What kind of deal?" I demanded.

"I'll tell you what I see in the
environment if you'll tell me the
underlying emotions in my fellow
Singers."

"You can't read their eyebands?" I
asked incredulously.

"I don't have a clue what you have
been reading, but I know you have
been able to clearly read my every
inner emotion and not once have
you ever been wrong. How do you do
it?"

"You really don't know?"

"If I really knew, why would I be asking?" The color was pink.

"Right now for example your face is severe, but you really are amused by this conversation--right?" I stated smugly.

"Right as right can be... What's the trick?"

"When you experience an emotion your eyebands change color. And the color increases with the depth of the emotion."

"What are you talking about?"

"I'm just saying that your eyebands change color. And I learned to interpret your colors."

"But my eyes never change color. The idea is preposterous."

"Do you trust the Grodatts to give you an honest answer?" I asked Tinkle. "And by the way, you are now fully experiencing annoyance." I said with a shrug of my shoulders.

"Mildleaf my good friend." Tinkle said with his tiniest bell-tone.

"You are feeling foolish," I chided. And now you are feeling annoyance again." I giggled.

Mildleaf came over to where we were sitting in the shade of a cocata tree. "There something I do for da good friend a Tink?" the large Grodatt said with his open simple face showing concern.

"Can you read the concern in his face?" I asked Tinkle.

"I don't find you that funny." Tinkle replied, and we both laughed.

"Be asked me come. What dat you want me?" the Mouser asked sensing that we had been laughing at his expense.

"I have a question for you. Would you help me with my problem good Mouser." Tinkle said, trying to unruffle the anger that was

obviously building in the proud
little policeman.

"Maybe I be-- Maybe I non-be. Me
not like jokin ta me. Not a
genlerman ting you be den. Me
thought dem Bha-ats be polite an
mannerly an..."

"We mean no harm. And I'm sorry
for my inconsiderate attitude," I
said, feeling particularly shitty.

"I Meant no insult....." Tinkle
said, his eyes purple.

"Den we touch," The Mouser said.

Tinkle and I both realized that
this was not a request. I placed
my arms around both Tinkle and
Mildleaf. Whatever Mildleaf needed
to know he must have found out
immediately, for he grinned and
the tension was gone. I realized
there and then that we all had our
means of understanding. The Bha-at
read minds. I read body language,
and it seemed the hugging little
Grodatts read body contact.

"Mildleaf. What color are my eyes?" Tinkle asked Mildleaf.

"Green an gold." came the immediate reply from the Mouser.

"And my body."

"Brown an gold. Yer sorrta the color big bumblers visit da fwa-Foo. Don't meanin insult, fer we o da Farthing love dem we does. Dey makes da plants happy dey does."

""I look like a bumble bee to you?" Tinkle said. His eyes just a touch on the orange side.

"Feel foolish?" I asked.

"Just a little ..."

"Well don't feel that way. I've always thought that both you and the Bhazz looked like giant bumblebees. We from earth have good feelings about bumblebees. And we have an inbuilt aversion for spiders. So it's hard for me to see you as the son of a spider."

The Windwalkers Of Xambic

"Did you see my eyes just change color?" Tinkle asked the Mouser, who wasn't sure what we were babbling about.

"No. You can't change color. Don't pull trickies on da Mouser. Dat not fer good buddy-guys dat trick."

"Seems that you are unique in your vision my earth friend," the Bha-at said with conviction.

"It will be our little secret."

"Buddy-guys. You be sneaky talkin. Member yer promised." And we hugged and our bond was made.

"What do you pick up Tinkle?" I asked.

"Whatever it is has a good defense. I'm hitting it with a vibra-4 level of penetration and its deflecting it easy."

"Then we know it's not a native," I said without thinking.

"Actually we know nothing of the kind. I know it isn't that Scram the Quick. And I know it isn't an adult Grodatt, because they are all here but whatever it is, has a very powerful shield."

"And you don't get any reading?" I asked.

"Funny thing... Even the best shield has some weakness that can be interpreted. While I can't make out the mind of the shield creator, there is lots of information regardless."

"Such as?" I asked.

"For openers, it's a blanket shield. That means that only one life force is putting up a shield to cover more than just itself." Tinkle said concentrating, his eyeband bright silver.

"Could it be using a blanket device to throw a reader off?" I asked, interested in learning more about the deductive process of the Bha-at.

A flash of pale yellow, quickly replaced by the soft pink of humor.

"You never quit probing ... Do you?" Tinkle asked.

"Guess not… But, that's what I do. After all I am a commander in the probe fleet and as such it's my nature to be interested in everything around me. If I ever lose my zest for learning—it's retirement for me."

"With all your interest in probing and solving questions, you must have a small interest in the earth game. Chesk."

"Chess." I corrected, "and as a matter of fact, it is a game that I love and miss dearly since my good friend TC bit the drink," I said, wondering what had been the fate for my crystal friend.

"TC... Bit the drink? What does this mean?" And the eyeband turned a silver-orange. By what I had learned already I knew that silver meant he was deep in thought, and usually the orange was a sign of feeling confused or foolish.

"Are you confused by what I said?" I asked.

"Just a little. You have never mentioned TC, chess, or this drink problem. I thought you were straightforward."

"I am. It's just that the subject has never come up. TC was my companion and navigator-pilot. When the probe splashed down in the sea it--it hit the drink... in Federation jargon. So you see, there is nothing complex, secret, nor mysterious. It was just not important enough to mention."

"Losing your companion was not important enough to mention?"

276

"TC is only a series of crystals. However intelligent she may have been-- she was only synthetic crystals."

"And that makes her less of a being to you."

"Hey! C'mon what is this third degree about anyway? We are only talking about a machine," I defended.

"I think not." Tinkle gave me the ruby-red eye.

"Touch now... Sick inside not good. Touch to me. Touch to me." Boozy Bentleaf said, hugging me, then quickly hugging Tinkle.

"Good friend to each and other we be now. We fella touch, den dat hurt be gone... Hug!"

And suddenly the Grodatts were all hugging us and each other, forming a tight-knit group.

"We all good-buddy fellas, this place. Soon, we be safe at the

Farthing. Den dis booger ina rockpile go way. You see!"

How could they know I wondered, and I could see by the bright silver that Tinkle was also deep in thought.

"You humans are strange." Tinkle said, with warmth.

"How so?" I asked.

"With one statement you refer to this TC as being nothing more than a robot, then with the next breath you are referring to it as... Her! Doesn't that seem strange to you?"

"No, for on our home planet we think of ships and countries and even the planet itself as being... Her. With us it has no hidden meanings." I said without thinking.

"Are you sure?" came the melodious challenge.

"Hard to be sure of something that has been taken for granted for as long as we have. It is not something we even think about. It's just like breathing for us, we just do it. It really doesn't require thinking about," I said, starting to think about it for the first time ever.

"When we get back to the farthing we should see if we can make a chess set." Tinkle said, changing the subject.

"Yes, I would enjoy ripping your brains out," I grinned.

"We'll see who does the ripping... friend." --Gold eyes.

Tinkle was now getting some very strong vibrations from the rocky ridge that was directly to the north of us. The ridge was to the north and the sea was to the south. We had to travel west to return to the Farthing. Whatever had followed us for the past two days seemed reluctant to come out of the rocks and into the white sand. We hugged the water line not wanting to get any closer to the shielded entity.

"Do you think it's hostile?" I asked Tinkle.

"Can't tell. Only thing I can deduce is that there is more than one being under the shield, and by observation alone it seems obvious that it is not interested in making contact."

"But it is definitely interested otherwise it wouldn't be following us." I replied.

"True. And then we have to factor in the panic it is creating in these normally everbold comalongs. I remember these creatures had absolutely no fear of the Mothers and not many living things in this Galaxy are comfortable around the powerful auras the mothers splash-broadcast." admitted Tinkle.

"Hopefully the rock ridge doesn't cross our path." I said, then I remembered that we had to spend almost a full day on the rocky ridges.

"I can see by your face that you remember that we have at least a day on the ridges." Tinkle said softly.

"Not reading my mind are you?" I asked in an attempt at lightening the situation.

"Don't have to. Your face tells the story."

"Dat ting dats up ina rockpile surest be spooky to da comalongs, what you fellas tink dat ting be?" Mildleaf asked, with very deep concern.

"Whatever they are, they aren't interested in coming in for a tea." I said. Still attempting to keep the situation light.

That night we camped at the edge of the ridge. Not a member of our little party was interested in getting caught on the ridge in the dark.

"Tomorrow we start early and we should be back into the sand before sunset," I said.

And our little band slept as close as we could, and all through the night the comalongs woofed and warbled in anger and what I thought to be fear.

"Never be seeing da comalongs fraid a nuthin. Me never leave da Farthing no more." Ican said to the Mouser.

"Me tink you pretty smart Ican. Dem dat want ta wander can have my travel-trip. Me miss da homeplace. Me!" Mouser replied.

The morning took a long time coming and not a member of our party slept a wink. The comalongs spent most of the night woofing and warbling, and with the first light of day they became very active running out into the dunes warbling excitedly. Then suddenly retreating to our camp with much angry hooting.

The Windwalkers Of Xambic

Just as we broke camp and headed toward the nearest ridge, the sand around us boiled with hundreds of Sandvipers.

"Dirty boogers." Mildleaf said producing two small evil sneems.

All the other Grodatts produced small throwing stones. In other hands I would have laughed at the tiny stones but with the remembrance of the swamp. I knew these stones were lethal.

The comalongs tore into the advancing sandvipers ripping and tearing and leaving viper parts everywhere. And many vipers met a rock in the eye that ended the life of the foul creature. Tinkle and the Grodatts threw stones, while Mildleaf and I probed the sand with our sneems and tried to edge our small group out of the now dangerous sand. We had forgotten all about the threat from the ridge.

Just as we thought the comalongs
had the viper attack contained,
the monster viper of all vipers
raised its monstrous head from the
sand. It was easily sixty feet
long, and at least four feet in
diameter. Its venomous fangs were
longer than I was tall and its
yellow eyes gleamed with evil
intelligence. This was no dumb
snake. This was a thinking beast
with a purpose.

Several of the comalongs lost
control and attacked the beast,
they disappeared in its tunnel of
a mouth screaming in terror. The
Grodatts would have fled in every
direction if they had been able to
move.

Somehow the devil-snake had
paralyzed all of the Grodatts. I
moved towards the towering machine
of death. Tinkle the Bha-at was at
my side. I gave him my longer
sneem and we two former enemies,
moved with great fear into the

face of certain death.   The
comalongs formed a wall in front
of us, and as a unit we attacked
the giant viper.

Evil intelligence glowed down at
us. And terror was in our hearts
but we could move our limbs and we
forced our reluctant bodies
forward to meet the coiling evil.

"It's been a pleasure knowing you
Tinkle."

"And I have been the richer for
your prying friendship." came the
flat unmelodious reply, and his
eyeband was an electric blue that
I had never seen before.

"Swing to its left and I'll take
it from the right. Don't try for a
blow until it strikes, but when it
does-- ride the sneem into its
evil yellow eyes ...   It's our
only chance. Do you understand?" I
said harshly.

"I understand," came the feeble
reply.

The gargantuan serpent coiled, its hooded eyes locked on the two of us. It completely ignored the hooting comalongs and started its uncoiling. And I was the target!

From the ridge came a mighty twang that caused the air to buzz with its force. A crude arrow as tall as the Bha-at, and as thick as my arm thrummed through the air and buried itself in the mighty viper's body. The monster curled back upon itself and tried to pull out the tree-sized arrow. Another arrow struck it in mid body. The viper howled in rage and pain. Not a snake hiss but a painful howl of disbelief. The next arrow must have struck a vital organ, as a red-black fluid bubbled down its body and into the sand. Where the foul black fluid struck the sand, the sand broke into fire and burned with a terrible putrid stench. The brave comalongs and Tinkle and I fell back in awe, and in fear of being struck by the thrashing beast. Soon the white sand was a blazing inferno around the monster.

"What forces are loose here?" Tinkle asked, looking to me for an answer.

"Nature gone mad, I would guess but stay back for I feel that even a drop of that putrid gore would end our lives." I said, not believing the scene unfolding before my eyes.

"Grodatts Ho!" Came a bellow from behind a twenty foot boulder that sat a few scant feet from the rocky ridge. Then from behind the boulder a giant stepped out into the sand.

"Stay back. Let the foul beast thrash its horrible body fluids into the sand. Even a drop will kill," came a small voice.   A very strong voice but small.

The voice was not coming from the bow-carrying giant. No, it was

coming from his great brown
leather cloak that fell to his
massive knees.

"Bigbow put me down." the small
voice demanded.

The giant was about half the size
of the two that had saved me in
the swamp. Even so he was easily
ten feet tall. And his great bow
was as tall as himself. He smiled
a mouth-full-of-teeth smile that
caused the Grodatts to fall back.

"Sowwy," thundered the voice of
the small giant.

But when he had flashed his
incredibly white teeth-- I noticed
that unlike the larger Windwalkers
flat teeth... his teeth were
canine.

"What are his thoughts?" I asked
Tinkle.

"Not much!" Tinkle whispered. "but
the simple patterns he is putting
together are friendly."

"Yes, I don't get any hostile body language either. If it wasn't for those teeth I would wonder why he carries the bow."

"Good fortune for us that he carries it," Tinkle said.

The white haired giant reached inside his greatcloak and came out with a Twigg in his hand. "Put me down – son." the two footer ordered the hunter.

"I am Tata Windsoother, the Elder of all Windwalkers, and this is my son, Bigbow. Say hello Bigbow." the bearded Twigg said.

The giant placed the Blue Twigg gently on the sand.

"Hewow," grinned the giant, then, he quickly put his massive hand over his mouth to hide his teeth. But his eyes were alight with merriment and it didn't take a student of body languages to see that this giant was both simple and very very friendly.

"Sowwy bout the teef Tata, but I forgets," came the friendly boom of apology. This set the Grodatts into action and soon the Giant was being swarmed with hugging Grodatts.

"I wikes these peepl Tata."

"And these people like you Son," beamed the blue Twigg.

And indeed we all did, for without the deadly archery of this magnificent hunter we would all be dying in agony.

I had a feeling that from this day forward that this giant would be ever welcome in the village of the Grodatts and in their hearts as well. Somewhere a Grodatt was already singing a tune about the evil demon, and the greatness of Bigbow the hunter.

We all listened as the tiny Grodatt strummed the tune.

"I weely likes them Tata," came the lisping voice from the great childlike hunter.

"Yes and now you will be able to visit them without frightening them half to death. Never again will you have to watch them from a distance my son." the Tata said with tears in his old eyes.

The crowd roared its approval. Someone suggested that Bigbow be given a Grodatt name. This ended in a heated dispute that waged for over a click around the giant who had seated himself on the sand so the little people could be closer to him. Like a great child he would reach out and touch a Grodatt ever so gently with his great finger, then he and the Grodatt touched would laugh in glee. I noticed that they quickly forgot about his teeth in their joy at having a new citizen of the Farthing.

"We decide da Grodatt name fer
Bigbow. Good Grodatt name. Name be
Bigheart. From now all houseys be
open to dis biggest Grodatt...

Every Grodatt screamed. "Bigheart
the Grodatt."

"Were our problem so simple."
Tinkle said with a gold-glow.

"It could be. And worse yet-- it
should be, for are we not more
intelligent than these simple
folk?" We both laughed but it was
not the laughter of happiness.
Rather, it was frightened
laughter, laughter that is heard
in a child's voice when singing
and laughing and whistling -- in
the dark.

"We thank you and your son for our
lives. But, that is quite obvious
how we feel," I said to the Blue
Twigg.

"Yes but somehow I can't believe
that the Grodatts are the
happiest. Look at the boy!" Tata

said. The giant had Grodatts in his lap, on his shoulders. One was even crawling up his heavy braided ponytail, with the intention of sitting on his head. For many years Bigbow has followed the little folk from a distance, always fascinated by them but I have never let him get close."

"Why not?" I asked

"I've always feared his frightening or accidentally hurting them. It would appear it is now out of my hands," Tata said, with wet eyes. "Now Winnie will have to let them be together," the blue Twigg said with determination.

Tinkle and I just looked at each other.

"Strange happenings are afoot." Tinkle said only for my ears. But Tata was listening.

"Strange, but good," I agreed.

The comalongs formed a circle around Bigbow, and one by one they approached the sitting giant and woofed three times then left to return to the circle. Not until every comalong had gone through this ritual did the others leave. When the final comalong had woofed its final woof and returned to the circle, only then did the circle break up. But even then, not before one final group woofing.

"Dey nebber done dat before." Mildleaf said impressed.

And as a group we headed towards the village of Grodatt. The Grodatts marched as a band around their bass drum and the bass drum was Bigbow. They sang happily, and it was as if a wandering brother had come home from the wars. Every now and then a Grodatt would be overcome, and rush forward to hug one of Bigbow's column-like legs. And this is how we returned to the village of Grodatt. Safely!

CROP FAILURE

We were one day out from the Farthing and settling in for the night. Overhead, the two moons glowed blue-gold, and the Mhyn was only a day's journey through territory familiar to the Grodatts.

Many small cook fires were burning cheerily and around each fire the Grodatts were smoking common peep-weed from the Digabouts. Tata Windsoother was happy in his anticipation of the piggot that roasted over a bed of coals. Tata's pointed little face was a bright red from his inspection of the succulent piggot.

"Is it not ready yet?" Tata asked Bigbow.

"Soon. Tata. Soon," the gentle giant grinned.

"Any interested in a helping of
the delectable...?" the little
elfin creature asked, already
knowing the answer.

Bobbing around the piggot in his
green finery, complete with
pointed hat and upturned slippers,
he was every inch the picture of a
tiny leprechaun hopping around his
pot of gold-- in glee.

I found a small stone a few feet
from the golden-brown piggot and
sat and watched the tiny elf-like
being turn the wooden pole that
the piggot was spitted on.

"Sure looks delicious," I said,
wondering how long before it would
be ready. My mouth was watering in
anticipation.

"Partake in a bit of the noble
beastie, would yee?" Tata said
with a wide grin that displayed
his small, flat teeth.

"Yea I could partake of the
victuals of such a delectable

beastie," I replied in the same artificial voice that he had asked in. And I'm sure my face had the same silly grin as his, as I had not eaten a roast of anything since arriving on Xambic, and the anticipation was almost unbearable.

Soon it was ready, and the giant tore it into three parts, the two smaller ones he wrapped in cocata fronds and passed one first to his father then one to me. He then sat with his back against a cocata and Tata climbed up onto the safety of his knee, clutching his huge rib of succulent piggot under his arm.

"Come sit on Bigbow's other knee. It will make the lad happy for the company, and you will be safe from a surprise by a dirty viper." Tata said, devouring his dinner with gusto.

Before I could reply the giant had gently scooped me up and deposited me on the other knee.

"Hard to imagine a viper approaching this camp. There must be at least a hundred comalongs around this camp," I said.

But Tata was not interested in talking, he was too occupied with his dinner. In spite of his diminutive size and small flat teeth he was a trencherman of no small ability.

Good eats?" the giant asked, his mouth full.

"Good eats!" I agreed heartily, my mouth also full. And so we spent the last night in the desert.

The following afternoon the Grodatts marched happily into the Farthing. With the problem of Galactic war between the Singers and the Nhark and Nyzan Dynasties still far from solved, I was not as joyful as the Grodatts.

Tinkle was quiet and by his constant shade of blue. I could

tell his emotions were running from worry to fear.

The village was empty, and if not for the Grunts attending the now dead gardens, there would have been only the odd wild milkathing and the odd morabat moving in the streets. Even the knabbit's who never left the gardens were not to be seen.

From the small door in the Mhyn came a running of children. Soon all the children that had been left in the tender care of Winnie were reunited with their parents.

Bigbow and Tata joined me with Muma Broadleaf in the cleaning up of the Wild Piggoty Inn. Bigbow went off into the desert in search of something to cook in the hearth and the village returned to normal... Normal if we didn't notice the Grunts digging and watering the little barren plots. Not a plant was to be seen.

After two days Dilbo came to live in the Wild Piggoty Inn with Bigbow and me. And Tata went to live in the Mhyn.

"How long since Tata has been in the village?" I asked Dilbo.

"I have never seen him here." Dilbo said.

After a week Tinkle came out of the Singer camp to visit.

"How are things in the Singer camp?" I asked.

"They are very bad. The Singers are weak and the Kha are running around like insane creatures terrified and confused by the strangeness of the Singers. Even the Bhazz are despondent, and not their aloof overbearing selves."

"And what do you propose can be done to return your people to your planet and let this planet return to its natural destiny without interference-- You still agree that this is the way?" I asked the dejected Bha-at.

"Certainly I agree that we should go home but I am not the ruler. The Khrii is confused and has no answers."

"What if the Khrii can formulate no solution?" I asked.

"Then the Mother Singers will declare Mother-law and take over all policy," Tinkle said bitterly

"What will be their policy?' Dilbo asked.

"Instant hostilities until the fwa-foo is growing again. The Mothers are aggressive enough when they have the fwa-foo but now that they are using only enough to function, they are functioning in a very mad fashion."

"How so?" Dilbo asked.

"Well for example they have ordered that all Grodatts be exterminated already.   And one

Mother ate a Khrx in her rage and anger. Only rarely has a Mother ever done this."

"Do you think the Khrii will give in and declare war?" I asked the blue eyed Bha-at.

"No. The Noble Khrii is intelligent enough to realize that if she allows the Grodatts to be exterminated the growth of the herb that allows the Mothers to transport will be a herb of the past. Then, we will never leave this planet. No, the Khrii will not allow war. At least she will allow no war-- while she lives."

"Is there any chance that the Singers would kill her?" I asked, watching Tinkle's eyeband carefully.

"No. They can't physically do her any damage, and the Khrx take no orders from anyone but a Bhazz."

"What about the Bhazz? Don't you think they will order an attack on the village?" Dilbo asked with concern.

"Never! For they are all as intelligent as their leader, and never would a Bhazz challenge a leader-Khrii, so there is no danger from the crazy old Mothers."

"What about the Singers overcoming the Khrii and all the other Bhazz with their psi-powers?" I asked.

Silver eyebands faced me. "Not a chance! The Bhazz have greater powers than the Singers."

"Then why don't they stop the Singers?" Dilbo challenged.

"Because the Singers are the Mothers!" Tinkle blurted, with just a shade of anger in his voice and eyeband.

"What of the Grunts?" I asked.

"What of the Grunts?" Tinkle said suspiciously.

"The way I see it the Grunts will obey the Singers, for they are easily manipulated by the songs the Singers sing."

"True," Tinkle said.

"Then we should be ready for an attack by the Grunts?" I asked Tinkle.

"You should be ready, but not overly concerned, as we are having trouble within our ranks." Tinkle said.

Tata and Winnie came towards us. They were talking quietly in a language I never expected to hear again.

"Are you speaking Xambic?" I asked not believing my ears.

"What do you know of Xambic?' Tata said turning to see if anyone else was listening.

"Come into the orchard it seems it's the only place that the Grunts have not ruined."

The Windwalkers Of Xambic

"I traveled many years ago with a little girl who was just becoming herself and she taught my friend TC Xambic."

"I never knew that any but the Old Ones spoke Xambic," muttered Tata.

"You speak it!" I challenged.

"Yes we do but then again you don't know who we are."

"Then enlighten me," I said reaching for a small yellow fruit from a vine.

"We are fulfilling a training period." Winnie spoke with a small tinkle.

"Then you are not natives to this planet?" I asked.

"Only the planet is native to itself throughout this universe. If you have walked with a Xambic speaker surely you are apprised of this basic fact." Tata said.

"Do you represent the RhaEve?" I asked bluntly.

"We represent ourself only."
Winnie said with a smile.

"You represent yourself? Don't you
mean you represent yourselves?" I
corrected.

"Have it your way," Tata said.

"No. I don't want it my way. I
want it the right way!" I said
with anger at what I thought was
deceit.

"We intend not to lead you astray
little man but for such as you
there are questions without
answers-- as there have always
been. For as long as your kind has
existed, they have always been
more troubled with the "Why" of
life as opposed to the harmonious
continuance of it." Winnie said,
with patience.

"And your kind is troubled with?"
I asked.

A smile flashed in the corners of
four small shiny eyes. And it
flashed as a single entity.

"I think I am getting into deep water here." I said quietly.

"And this frightens you?" came the soft reply from Tata.

"Yes. I have questions to ask. Questions that will help me on my mission and I think the direction we are proceeding in is a direction that is involving powers best left undisturbed."

"If you have questions that need answers we will endeavor to answer as honestly and truthfully as we are permitted." came the sincere voice of Winnie.

"Are you separate entities?" I blurted.

"All beings in the universe are separate, and one-- unto themselves. It is merely a perception of being," came the musical and highly amused voice of the being that flowed together as the blending of lights. They had become a single glowing entity. Throbbing with energy.

"Then you can't be the mother of Dilbo." I said, looking to Dilbo who slept against a tree.

"I am the mother within the family of little people but not in the sense that you think of a mother." came the voice inside my head.

"Who are you?" I demanded.

"You know the answer to that already. We are the being who tends the well and is guardian to The Tree of Life. You have met us in our other beforances."

"But you never came up from the well and RhaEve never permitted me to get too close. She told me your breath was the breath of life to some but it was the fog of death to all beings mortal," I said with conviction.

"And you believe yourself to be mortal?" came the amused voice inside my head.

"I am born of man." I challenged.

"Yes you were born of wo-man but then you walked with the RhaEve through her Garden and viewed the Old Ones. Do you not find it just a little strange that you lived by the lake for twenty thousand years on Rha, and then another thirty thousand working for the Federation? Not just a little strange and un-mortal?" came the voice.

"Our scientists have studied my metabolism and assure me that I could be killed as easily as any other human from my planet." I replied.

"While that is true. You are still over fifty thousand years old. Correct me if I'm wrong."

"No... You are correct." I admitted. "But, I would like an answer to my question."

"Repeat the question. For in your make up we see nothing but questions. Questions I might add that can't be answered, only asked and asked until the answer comes from within. Now repeat the question."

"Are you the parent of the Grodatts?"

"Come now-- look at us! You can see what we are and if you walked with the RhaEve you know our abilities-- and limitations, set down by the LAW. We have shown our trueform so that you can better address your own problems here. We know of your quest, but as much as we would like to help... The LAW is the LAW. We are only able to conduct our task within its limits."

"Then you deny creating the Grodatts?" I challenged.

Once more Tata was moving around in his little green suit, and Winnie was picking flowers in her flowing flowered frock.

"I must have fallen asleep," Dilbo said getting up.

"I wish I had." I laughed.

"Do you have any more questions?" Tata said sincerely.

"No. But. I do appreciate your honesty and I know the prime directive of the One Great Mother in her passing down the law that only the RhaEve can tamper with." I said, with angry resignation.

"And that law is?" Winnie said with a smile.

"No more games." I said, putting my hands over my head as if in surrender. "I know that you are restricted by a prime directive of the Tree but if you can help me in any small way, it will really be appreciated."

"We know--" came a voice in my head.

"Come and see the garden Tink." Dilbo said grabbing me by my sand-toned burnoose. As we walked toward the dead gardens. Dilbo asked me innocently, "What was Mom talking about?"

"Oh-- She was just playing games," I said.

"Sometimes she does that to me too," Dilbo said, and I could tell his innocent remark had been genuine.

"Halt!" ordered a surly Grunt.

"Nice garden." Dilbo grinned and we went to the Inn.

THE PROBLEM

The Wild Piggoty Inn was filled
with kakleberry hounds, and Muma
Broadleaf was serving the steaming
beverage to a familiar face. The
face belonged to Scram the Smart.

I cut directly through the crowd.

"I am here to explain." Scram said
nervous about my intentions.

"Relax. I have been told by an
unchallengable source that you
left me for my own good. However,
I have a raft of questions for you
to answer," I said. "Do you mind
if I sit with you?"

"Be my guest. I can anticipate
your questions and I think that
indirectly we are both working
towards the same goal."

"If you represent who I believe
you do, how is it that you have

been saddled with a fragile body?"
I asked.

"It is a vehicle not of my
choosing but it is a form that has
been given to me from the Guardian
of this Galaxy and although I
would have preferred to move
through the fabric of this small
Galaxy in a more flexible and
certainly more durable body, this
one was selected, and this one I
am stuck with." came the reply
from Scram.

"Then you are as vulnerable as any
of us?"

"Until I solve the riddle of this
weird planet. I'm limited to the
abilities and shortcomings of this
body." It seems that my
supervising Guardian believes--
that by having an emotional
involvement, and by being
vulnerable as any others in this
fabric, I will be very careful in
not rending the fabric."

"You are telling me you could lose your life if you make a mistake?" I asked.

"So it would seem. Seems the Guardian in this sector believes that if field agents are vulnerable themselves they will be more careful about wielding powers indiscriminately."

"Then you do have the ability to make changes?" I asked.

"No. Not anymore. The RhaEve is the only one that can affect a difference in the fabric of a happening. I am merely an observer that has an opening in the time fabric to slip through."

"I don't envy you your position. Now I have a question that has been bothering me.

"About the Twiggs?" and the grin was real.

"Yes-- About the Twiggs. What the hell are they?"

"Oh they are pretty much as you see them, and that's the problem. They are really a team of genetic engineers that have taken on two separate identities, and this proclivity for self-identity has destroyed their impartiality."

"You mean they have become too involved in the picture to see it clearly and make the proper adjustments?" I asked.

"Worse than that, they have become part of the picture."

"Then they are malfunctioning?"

"They seem to have become part of the problem, as part of the team has identified with the Windwalkers, and the other part has decided that it is a Mother of all the Grodatts."

"Then you were sent here to investigate them?" I asked.

"Actually I was sent to try and influence the Genetic mess the two races known as Kha are in."

"I don't think I understand." I said. Actually I had my opinions about the weird culture, but after fifty thousand years of being involved with so many divergent races I no longer really became that interested, other than an impartial observer.

"Well it seems that originally they were two distinctive races, the Singers being composed of the Mothers, the Kha, the working Khrx. This is a fairly common type genetic order, and it works well for all involved. You with me?"

"Sure! Each race is prevented from becoming a Galactic nuisance by their built in limitations." I replied.

"Good... You have the concept. In the past there were two separate races and somehow they were able to alter their genes. One race was known as the Kha and the other the Bha-at"

"Making one race from the two?" I asked.

"That's it. Now that would have not been a problem if neither race was warlike.   But because the completely unambitious Bha-at genes were dominated by the malevolent nature of the Singers-- We have a problem in this sector." Scram said, stopping to eat a slice of hot bread, just brought with his kakleberry.

"What is the solution?" I asked.

"It seems the solution is to have the Bha-at males regain their lust for the Bha-at females."

"It can't be that simple." I said thinking about his proposed solution.

"Actually it is, for the Mother-Singers remove egg cells from young Bha-at females. They fertilize them with sperm taken from the Bha-at males and they incubate them internally."

"The Singers can do that." I said in wonder of it.

"The Singers could be gene-mothers to any species,"

"Even humans?" I asked with a shudder.

"Even humans-- be careful about getting yourself in the picture Marples, for to do so will bias your concept of what is transpiring right under your nose."

"Okay....Okay!" I said shuddering. Then the Bha-ats are still intact as a species?"

"Sure, the only damage that has been done is that they think of themselves as Singers. When the truth is that the two species are totally alien to each other." Scram said.

"How so?" I asked, not sure of what two species they actually were before the joining."

"The truth of the matter is that the Kha are Arachnids and the Bha-at are of the genus Bombus." Scram told me.

"Bombus?" I repeated, not believing my ears.

"Bombus." Scram repeated with a straight face, but I could see he was watching for my reaction.

"Bombus and Arachnid in one nest?"

"That's the long and short of it."

"Bumblebees and spiders... Brothers and sisters in one nest! It just can't be," I said, flabbergasted.

"Marples, I guarantee it to be the truth."

"As I remember the bumblebee queens give birth to workers, and the workers give birth to the males. Is that not correct?" I asked not needing an answer.

320

"True but we are not talking about your earth bumblebees. We are talking about a highly evolved genus of Bombus."

"How do they differ? Other than in size and intellect?" I asked, not knowing the answer.

"For openers-- they mate directly and live as a family unit, with the mother being the queen of their household-- and the male the adoring slave-husband."

"Not too different to humans," I laughed, "but what about the children? What about them?"

"Just like humans, male-female, with no distinction other than their sex."

"But look at the difference in size."

"What about it?" Scram said, without interest.

"Well the Bhazz are twice as big as the males, and about fifty times more aggressive"

"That has nothing to do with the Singers. They are only guilty of keeping the Bombus population small, and brainwashed."

"By brainwashing them. I guess you are referring to the Bombus thinking of themselves as Kha instead of Bha-at." I said.

"That, and suppressing the male-female desire in the embryonic stage."

"Then if the male-female lust factor was regained-- the Bombus would return to normal?" I asked.

"I hope so-- for my assignment is to turn this situation around, and I am stuck on this uncivilized waterball until I finish this assignment." Scram said wistfully.

"You sound like you're burned out."

The Windwalkers Of Xambic

"Burned out and ready for retirement. This is my last assignment."

"Why did you choose to affect a change here instead of on their home planet?" I asked. "I gather you are a city dweller and Kha is a highly civilized planet. It seems you would have enjoyed your assignment under circumstances more to your liking."

"Truthfully I would have selected Kha but there the order of social niceties are so strongly enforced I would never be able to achieve my task," Scram said, turning and ordering another carafe of kakleberry.

"You had better take it easy on the Kakleberry, or you will not achieve anything other than becoming a sot."

"And that bothers you?"

"Not much as it has nothing to do with my reason for being here. My

job is pure and simple-- find out
if this sector has any problems
and report them to the fleet. I've
found the problem and now I can't
get off this planet."

"If you're hinting at the use of
my electro-mag-grav capsule,
forget it! It is designed for my
metabolism and it would kill you
to enter it," Scram said through
bleary eyes.

"Agitation... Aggravation-and
Manipulation, are my stock in
trade ... Works every time," Scram
said with a wink and fell face
down on the table drunk as a
skunk.

Jeez. I thought to myself the
freedom of a whole race depends on
the actions of a drunk... Jeez!

"Your friend is enjoying himself!"
came a humorous voice from behind
me. I turned and looked to the
familiar face.

"Kookerman!" I said just a little too loud, as many conversations stopped, and many eyes were upon us.

"Well if you meant to have the whole tavern watching us, you are a great success," Kookerman purred, mischeviously.

"So it would seem." I replied quietly feeling stupid.

"Have you and the spy resolved your differences?" Kookerman whispered, his large, intelligent eyes ablaze with mischief.

"My business hardly seems your business," I said, angrily.

"Ahhaa! So you still harbor ill tidings for my deserting you in the desert." he whispered, without a touch of regret in his great electric-black eyes. Eyes dancing with amusement.

"I don't find it as funny as you do. You left me to die, and now you sit and make jokes. I think

you are not as funny as you seem
to think you are. But then again
I've seen the mighty prince of
Nyzerbad under fire" I said with
heat.

"I left you not to die! ... Little
man! For me to have remained would
have been certain death for you."

"Sure!" I said taking a drink from
my small glass and ignoring
Kookerman. "Some prince!" I
muttered quietly.

With a swoop of his great-- almost
living cloak, he was in the seat
across from me.

"I will speak and you will listen.
Then if you still feel betrayed--
there is nothing I can do but
first you must listen."

I listened and soon I realized
that if he would have stayed a
terrible blood bath would have
occurred in the desert, and it
would have been one he could have
extricated himself from, but one

that would have left me at the mercy of blood-crazed fools.

"Okay! So you didn't have a choice." I admitted.

"That's not good enough! Understand clearly that I did have a choice but one that left you dead... And I chose to leave you alive! Do you understand!" Kookerman hissed with such force that the whole tavern shuddered under the impact of his voice.

"Yeah, we all do." I said. Then I laughed.

Kookerman didn't laugh but reached across the table and his massive hand swallowed my hand and half of my lower arm.

"Friends?" He said with extreme sincerity.

"I don't know," I said with equal sincerity.

"Not enemies?" he continued with an obvious need to resolve our difference.

"No... No. I don't think we are."

"Good!" He hissed and left the Inn-- like a great-black-bird of prey. The crowded Inn shuddered as he passed through the door.

"What did that monster want?" Dilbo asked, talking quietly, so as not to waken the drunken Scram.

"Wants to be friends." I said.

"Gots to be careful bout ceptin frens like dat guy," the Mouser said, wisely.

"We have private matters that we must discuss," Dilbo said, with a grave look on his normally happy face.

FACING THE SPIDERS

We headed to the now abandoned garden of Dilbo.

"We must rid ourselves of these pesky spiders." Dilbo said bending down and taking a handful of soil and examining it carefully. "It will take months for this good soil to heal from the alien things that the Grunts have put in it."

"All the fwa-foo patches are the same. Fortunately they have left the veggies and orchard alone." Mildleaf the Mouser said.

"What did you want to talk about?" I asked Dilbo.

"I want to know if you are going to help?"

"Help what?"

"Help us fight the Singers. Isn't that why you came to Xambic?"

Dilbo asked, watching me for a reaction.

"No. I didn't land on purpose. I was really only investigating the complaints of lost shipping in this area."

"In other words-- Xambic zamed ya." Dilbo said, smiling.

"Real funny," I answered, not returning his smile.

As we considered our options, they were quickly to become only options of retreat, for the Khrx and Grunts were already on the way to the village with highly sophisticated weapons designed on Kha. Weapons that would function on Xambic!

As the army advanced, the Grodatts retreated to the Mhyn. From high in the grow-room-observatory, every Grodatt from the Farthing of Longbottom peered down at the thousands of massed soldiers below.

The Windwalkers Of Xambic

"You are a soldier of the federation," Dilbo said.

"What is our first move?"

"From what I can see down there, we have exactly no moves."

"There must be something we can do." Dilbo said.

"Our only chance is to get help. Do you have powers of war that I am unaware of?" I watched Winnie carefully.

"I think you know better. As you have already surmised, I have already stepped beyond my allowable involvement."

Even as we spoke, Scram had planted the seed of truth in the Bha-at and both the female Bhazz and the male Bha-at were presently confronting the Mother-Singers with the deception that had been perpetrated on the Kha-at for thousands of years.

Being that there was only a hundred of the female warriors, and they had little chance of declaring war on the thousands of heavily armed warriors that surrounded the Arachnid Mothers. Realizing their situation, the small band of Bombus warriors struck quickly and escaped with their males.

Even as we spoke, they were headed for the village of Digaboot. The party was led by Tinkle. Tinkle, who knew that help was needed in overcoming the superior forces of the heavily armed war-party of Grunts and Khrx. A few Bhazz and fewer Bha-at had not believed Scram and had remained faithful to the Singers.   Only because they still believed themselves to be of the Kha family and not of the Bha-at family.

After a week of being shut in by the army camped on the door-step of Mhyn-- we planned an escape.

And then as if in anticipation of our escape, the Grunts plugged the single door with rocks and clayed it in. This not being enough of an insult they built great fires baking the clay into a cement.

In front of the face they hauled flat rocks daily, and then packed clay between the rocks. Soon the sun had baked this into a smooth surface impossible for the Sandshrieks to penetrate.

"They really have us cemented in. Is there no other exit from this fortress?" I asked Winnie.

"None that any here could use," Winnie said with finality.

As soon as the cemented plaza was baked to a stone finish the Singers were carted in on their wagons.

"Now we have the despicable creatures right in our face. They mean to stay here until we starve to death," Dilbo said with great anger. "We could chip away the opening." he continued.

"No. Without help we are finished. But we still have enough supplies for at least a month. All we can do is hope for help," I said to Dilbo.

"From who?" Dilbo asked, without hope.

"From wherever it may come, Winnie said softly. Another week passed without help.

We were starting to consider chipping away the door and facing the Khrx and Grunts in a suicide attack, when on the horizon we spotted four dirty airbags.

"It's Augustus Fung" Dilbo burst out. "I'd never have believed that I'd be happy to see that fool airhead."

"An look at dat!" Mildleaf yelled," must be all da waterheads!"

The Windwalkers Of Xambic

Coming into the bay was a flotilla
of thousands of boats. One man
boats, two man boats, and what
looked like piles of flotsam with
lateen sails. The bay was filling
with vessels that defied
description. And, as ugly and
filthy as they were, they brought
joy for us trapped in the Mhyn.

Mildleaf and Boozy Bentleaf
immediately set about chipping the
doorway free. Soon the doorway was
a boiling, singing throng of
chippers.

The airbags had small fires in
sandstone fireboxes. Each balloon
was equipped with rudder and
windscrew, and in spite of their
decrepit look, they followed a
direct path that was soon to take
them directly over the army below.
Meanwhile, the confused Grunts and
even stupider Khrx were in need of
direction. The few Bhazz that had
remained were running back and
forth, madly issuing orders to the

Bha-at, who were even fewer in number. Everywhere was confusion.

But not in the skies!

With a swoop, the first airbag dipped in and made a direct pass over the 666 Tetrahedron web. When directly overhead, clay amphoras were hurled down at the Singers and the Web.

Each amphora had a burning wick that ignited the pitch and oil contents of the jars. Fires were everywhere. Everywhere-- but on the web. Arrows filled the air and the airbags rose out of range, but they continued their passes with an incredible dexterity and control that was our joy to behold.

Meanwhile, the armada was landing its contents. Islanders that attacked with a frenzy. I could see that at least thirty star clusters had had shipwrecks on this strange planet, for the attackers represented almost every culture in the Galaxy. And I noticed two boatloads of attackers that were not known to me, which meant they were from outside of our Galaxy. I made a note to find out where they were from, and what kind of drive unit they possessed that would enable them to travel from one Galaxy to another. As far as I knew, only the Old Ones had the ability for intergalactic travel.

Out of the desert came the entire village of Digaboot. Shovels and rakes and hoes-- in the place of spears and sneems. With the Digabouts, came a herd of woofing comalongs and in the middle of the sea of chaos could be seen-- two black cloaked warriors-- mowing down everything in their path.

Soon, angry Grodatts were out and swarming into the fight.

Everywhere, and in every direction the Grunts and Khrx could be seen beating a retreat. Then they would hold the line, and surge back to recapture the camp. The last surge by the Singer forces looked to leave them in control of the camp.

Suddenly, with a great thrumming and drumming, a band of at least a hundred great beasts at least twenty feet tall came out of the desert. Their terrible voices rumbled. "Tonight we dine on roasted Grunts-- Grunts. Grunts. Grunts!" Then the terrible beasts beat their wicked stone axes against massive wooden shields. "And for breakfast we dine on boiled Khrx," they roared in unison.

Without their Bhazz to organize and control their formations, the Kha forces fled in fear, but keeping the Singer wagons deep in their midst. Not one Singer had been damaged, but they had been driven from the village of Longbottom at great cost to their army. And the web was destroyed.

The Windwalkers Of Xambic

I noticed that the Bhazz-- who had earlier been told of their real heritage, by Scram the Manipulater, had not attacked the camp. And I could not blame them.

The combined forces that had just vanquished the Singer army spent the entire night burying the dead. And nowhere could be seen the great beasts that had turned the tide of battle.

"Where have the giants gone?" I asked Nyzerbad.

"They are right behind you, little man," Nyzerbad purred.

I turned to face only his queen, and the two ragtag boys that Nhioby had befriended.

"You mean that the mind bending Singers were put to rout by a simple hologram?"

"Tis poetic justice," Nyzerbad whispered, and his great black eyes shone with pride. "My lovely Nhioby has met them all in their own filthy arena of mind-interference, and my love has bested them at their own game."

"I noticed that you and Leklunc did more than your share in the arena of war." I said, genuinely having been impressed with the terrible paths of destruction the two had inflicted on the much larger forces of the Singer army.

"We affected little, it was my noble lady that made the difference," Nyzerbad said, in a voice brimming with pride for his lovely queen.

Small tents were being pitched everywhere, and the Grodatts and Digabouts were busy removing the stones and baked clay.

"Hateful creatures. They make everything unnatural," Dilbo said, to me, as he dug out a flat stone.

As the stones were removed from the clean, white sand, the busy Digabouts set up tents. Tents that looked more like mushrooms growing out of the sand, than they did places to sleep in.

Everywhere, cookfires were being started. And soon the armada had erected their colorful tents and the white sand was a patchwork of drabness and brilliance. Side by side, the Waterheads and the Digabouts set about cooking supper from the wealth of food the armada of stickboats had brought.

"We uns be meetin again, How be yer" came a familiar huffing and puffing.

"Admiral MaQuig, your navy was magnificent," I said, shaking his outstretched hand.

"You remember my officers?"" He said, obviously hoping that I had forgotten them, so he could lord their insignificance over them.

Flubby, Meryl, and Kenny stood with long faces, until I greeted them all by name-- as I would a relative, hugging each of them in turn.

Grodatt's, Digabouts, Airfolk, Watermen and all the other offworlders spent the next week celebrating the retreat of the Singers. Noticeably, was the absence of the Winnie-the-Twigg and the giant Windwalkers. Tata Windsoother on the other hand was in his glory, riding around in the pocket of Bigbow.

The party lasted for over a week before the food supplies started to run low.

"We be gettin ready fer home. As admural o all the navy. I be offerin rides ta all yer airfolk," MaQuig told Fung.

"Sorta low on pitch for the airships. Think we be ceptin yer most gracious offer. What say you airfolk?"

To a man they agreed for a ride home.

The Windwalkers Of Xambic

Soon all the airfolks were rafted and the motley crew set sail.

The Digabouts headed out on foot and soon the village of Grodatt was returned to uneventful bliss for the little people.

Dilbo brought clones from the one tree that grew in the dome top of Mhyn. And soon all the little gardens were once more emerald with new, vigorous growth. The knabbits moved back into the gardens to protect the plants from the leaf eating morabats.

"Looks like the dirty spiders are not going to be a problem anymore." Dilbo said, as we sat playing chess.

"They are not the problem here my good friend." I told Dilbo.

"Then why are you here? You are a trouble shooter. Or are you still sticking to that lame story of being an observer?"

"It's not a story Dilbo. I am an observer."

"And what about Scram? Is he an observer too?"

"Yes. I would say that if he has any powers, they are only powers of self escape," I replied.

"Nothing more?" Dilbo asked coyly.

"Nothing more." I replied, more interested in the strange ball game that was about to take place in the village square.

Two teams of four players to a team had set up a diamond almost identical to an earth baseball diamond. At each base they had driven two cocato stakes into the ground, then weaved fronds between the two small stakes.

"What are the fronds for?" I asked Dilbo.

"Thems ta hidin a runner," Mildleaf grinned. "Thought yer Earthies was ball-playerses."

The Windwalkers Of Xambic

"Check your queen!" Tata Windsoother exclaimed triumphantly.

"Check my queen?" I said looking from the ball field to our board.

"You can't check my queen," I laughed.

"I'm a-checking it anyhows!" gloated Tata.

"Tata's got his queen sure nuff!" Boozy Bentleaf said.

"If you take my queen, you'll be checkmated by leaving my knight free to mate your king.

They all laughed. Tata took my queen and I mated him.

"Checkmate." I said.

"Checkmate!" they roared in unison.

"Can't checkmate nuthin without yer queen," Boozy giggled.

"Thought you Earthies was s'posed ta be chessers. I be thinkin yer

needs lessons ta tha game proper-
like. We be havin lotsa time ta
teach yer, bein yer wants ta learn
proper chess. Does yer wanta?"
Boozy asked seriously.

"Where are the bats and the
gloves?" I asked, changing the
subject.

"Bats?" came the question from
Dilbo.

"What's a glove?" Boozy asked

"I got good idea ...You learn
Dattball ...You wanta be Ump?"

"I can't officiate a game that I
don't even know."

"How come?" Boozy asked clearly
confused by my answer.

"Well it just makes sense that you
must know the rules if you are
going to officiate a game." I told
Boozy.

"Don't need ter know rules."
Mildleaf put in.

"Why not?" I asked.

"Players know rules." Mildleaf offered, as if to an idiot.

"Then why do you need an Ump?" I asked Mildleaf.

"Players can't tell who won. Them that plays can't know who be winner. Got to be notplayer to be Ump."

"And I don't need to know the rules?"

"You see... You see..." they all laughed.

And so I became the umpire of Dattball.

First off, I was asked to make sure that each player only carried four rotten eggs. They did. Then I was told to tell the eight of them to "PLAY BALL!" and they started by four of them walking out to the square pitcher's mound. The other four hid behind the blind they called homeplate.

347

The four pitchers stood back to back, so that each pitcher was facing the space between bases.

"Strike one!" yelled the pitcher.

And one of the battless batters ran.

As the runner ran for the small, fronded, first base-- the pitcher tried to hit him. And the runner tried to hit any of the pitchers in the pitchers square.

They were both only allowed one of their four eggs.

With the runner safely hidden behind first base, the pitcher yelled, "Strike two," and the second runner tried for first, and the runner on first went for second. And then, both pitchers tried to nail their runner with an egg, and the two runners tried for any of the four pitchers. Agghhh! What a stupid game, I thought to myself.

348

At about this point on a mission, thoughts of home, complete with Candlestick Park and maybe a char-broiled... Ah well!

"What's the point to your game?" I asked Dilbo.

"To find out who is the best," Dilbo said, looking at me as if I was more than just a little simple. "You earthies are known to be great followers of the noble game of ball. Or is that in your history only?"

"No, we still enjoy a good game of hardball."

"Then why are you not enjoying yourself? You have talked a great deal about baseball and chess, yet, I feel you are not interested in our games. Am I correct?" Dilbo asked.

"I guess I'm ready for home. Don't look so sad Dilbo."

The four runners had all made it to home plate. Each player was given four more eggs and the runners and pitchers switched positions. And they repeated the senseless ordeal.

"How can you tell who wins?" I asked Dilbo.

"How can you tell who wins your games?" Dilbo challenged in reply to my question.

"It's pretty simple-- the umpire controls the game, and the team with the most runs wins," I said, bored with their game.

"That means that as soon as the game is over... That's it? You can't tell who won? Or who lost?" Dilbo asked.

"Well no..." I started to say.

"We can tell from game to game who the winners are!" Dilbo said and the Groddats all laughed good naturedly.

"I suppose you could smell them for a week," I admitted.

The Windwalkers Of Xambic

"Only the losers!" Boozy Bentleaf
cackled.

Again the Grodatts roared and not
at my expense.

"Dattball pretty honest game. What
you say?" Boozy asked.

"I say you're right," I conceded
with a smile, being sure to smile
with my mouth shut.

The game came to an end, and as
the umpire I was called upon to
sniff out the losers.

"Now you official Ump!" Mildleaf
said, proud of me.

I on the other hand was ready for
home, but I had accomplished
exactly nothing. The problem was
still unsolved. Someone--
Something was tampering with this
planet, and it was my mission to
stop it. So far I had not even
found out the culprit, never mind
stopping the action.

I was feeling hopeless, helpless
and in fact outright stupid and
incompetent without my friend TC.
For as long as I could remember TC
had been there with her incredible
support. I had always taken her
memory and intelligence for
granted, and here I was on my own-
- for the first time in longer
than I could remember. And I was
in trouble! I had a problem to
solve, and I had no idea where to
begin looking.

"Feelin alone?" Tata Windsoother
asked, touching my arm.

"Reading my mind?" I asked,
defensively.

"Hardly required. You are one
forlorn looking fella. And I don't
read minds. Tisn't polite."

Tata and I talked long into the
night. And the chess games waged
between the Groddats. Somehow,
after talking to the little dwarf-
like gentleman for clicks, the
ball game made more sense, and

even their wacky chess rules made sense. I could understand their reasoning, that even in chess-- a kingdom without a queen was one that could not continue-- for who would bear the royal children to continue the line? Everything they did made sense after talking to the little blue man for clicks.

I knew I was in trouble when everything he said started to make sense.

DILBO IS SUSPECT

The Singers showed little interest in leaving their new encampment. And life returned to normal.

"Want a game of chesser?" Dilbo asked.

"Nah. Gives me a terrible headache. As a matter of fact I have been noticing that any time I get involved with a problem requiring the application of mind, my head starts to ache."

"Really?" Dilbo replied, looking at me very strangely.

"When did it start?" Dilbo asked, watching me very closely.

"It started not long after I landed. I've got a theory, but nothing to really support it. So I'll pass up the game. Even now I feel a mild throb."

"Why didn't you mention it to me before?"

"Because I figured it to be some form of migraine, besides there is nothing you could do about me having a headache-- Is there?" I said, watching Dilbo for reaction.

His reaction was a slight discomfort, and this puzzled me. Why should my good friend Dilbo be in discomfort for something that he had nothing to do with? Could it be merely his sympathy for a friend? Or his being an empath and also feeling the... No, that made no sense, for if it was empathic he would have long sensed my pain and it would not be news.

Then why pretend that it was something he knew nothing about? While sorting this out in my mind, I had been staring at Dilbo but without seeing him as my mind was turned inward.

"Why are you staring at me?" Dilbo spluttered.

"I'm not staring, but now that you mention it you look guilty. What can you possibly feel guilty about Dilbo? Can it be you have something to do with my headache?"

"That's crazy," Dilbo replied in annoyance.

"It is isn't it? Why would you want to give me a headache? Then again why would anyone want to give me a headache?"

"Beats me." Dilbo replied once more his normal self.

"Well I'm tired of it beating me, and if someone doesn't solve this problem I'll be marooned here forever."

"Would that be so bad?"

"Not if I had a normal life span"

"How old are you?" Dilbo asked.

"Over four thousand earth years."

"And that is old?"

"By our standards it is. But I'm sure you already know the answer. Your library is immense. I would think that it has taken a great deal of time to collect so many books."

Dilbo laughed out loud and so did I. However, I noticed that he did not look amused. Not the slighest...

"What do you have in mind?" Dilbo asked.

"I think that wait and see is a game I can't afford."

"Why not?" Dilbo asked.

"Because I am forgetting what I have always known, and without TC to overcome my learning disability ... Soon my lack of retention and my inability to recall information will leave me no brighter than the Waterheads and Airbaggers."

"That's not possible!" Dilbo said, showing deep concern and worry. He even looked a bit guilty. Why guilt, I wondered.

"Can't you control your memory loss?"

"TC is my control, and without her replacing lost information, I will soon remember very little. And without information to work with, a mind is no better than a computer without software."

"What if we could find TC?"

"She splashed down miles from shore. I don't think there are any chances of finding her... Not without real technology."

"Maybe a Windwalker could find TC?"

"And how would we go about finding a Windwalker?" I asked.

My suspicion made Dilbo laugh.

"Yes I suppose that to suggest that I have any way of communicating with a Windwalker would have far ranging implications."

"Far ranging indeed." I replied without humor. "Anyway, before I forget who I am, and what my mission was-- I had better make a solid plan of action-- before I'm unable to do so."

"I can see that you are troubled deeply but you must believe I would never do you any harm, and you must believe that I will do whatever I can to help," Dilbo said.

"Define help," I said grinning.

"For openers I could call to order all sentients on Xambic and then we could hold what you call a court."

"And?" I asked, watching Dilbo closely.

"And you could ask them questions. And with your ability to read body-language, I'm sure you could tell if there was any deception or not. Is this not true?"

"True, I do have a small talent for reading. Even so, what will this avail me if there is nothing we can do to overcome the power of intelligence so powerful as to destroy an untamperable Q-class star probe. Also, Nhioby and Nyzerbad are very formidable and they are as helpless as I am."

"All true! But to identify your opponent is at least a start. By your own admission, each day leaves you with less gray matter to call on."

"What is your plan?" I asked.

"We could call a Great Gathering."

"What is a Great Gathering?"

"It is a calling all sentients are compelled to respond to."

"All sentients? Even the Singers?" I asked.

"Yes, all thinking life forces on Xambic must respond to the call of Mhyn."

The Windwalkers Of Xambic

"No exceptions?"

"No."

"How do you know this?" I said, thinking there was no reason to call anyone. For if Dilbo could call all the beings together on Xambic and they had to respond without volition... I had my culprit in hand.

"Come, I see much distrust in your face." Dilbo said, amused. Together we trod to his home in the heart of the mountain known as Mhyn.

"Haven't seen your mother lately," I said innocently.

"No. Mother has gone to her people. She is over-sensitive to strife and is unable to bear the pain without the ghlaming."

"I could use a little ghlaming with TC."

"Yes I suppose you could, but, there may be a way to salvage your

ship. But, that is too much for
me. Perhaps in the Great Gathering
someone will find a way. After
all-- if one mind is better than
two, think of the advantage of a
whole planet trying to solve a
problem." Dilbo said, then he
pointed to the shimmering wall.
"See the Rhunnicca on the wall?"

"I see it, but it is alien to me."
I answered Dilbo.

"You must put your hand on the
Rhunstone, then look at the wall
and think of nothing other than
the Rhunnicca." Dilbo said.

I approached the mushroom shaped
stone that grew out of the floor,
and put both hands on it. The wall
slowly started to shimmer and the
writing lost its shape. The harder
I concentrated on reading it, the
more it shimmered.

"Don't try so hard. You are trying
to see things written. Just relax
and it will come."

The Windwalkers Of Xambic

Soon the wall became a living map of Xambic. And I could feel that my thoughts were being sent to all living beings on this strange planet.

And I knew also that they would be able to respond to my calling of a gathering, or they could not bother, and always the choice to respond or not would be their choice. The device was merely a thought powered radio that needed no receivers. None other than sentients.

Who had originally used this device? And why?

"Well if your thoughts about me being the culprit were of any validity, you are now a fellow culprit." Dilbo said

"Point made. It's obvious this devise is older than old, and it is merely a broadcasting device. I wonder who made it?"

"Why would you suppose that someone made it?" Dilbo replied smiling. "Couldn't it be a natural phenomena?"

"I guess... But why?"

"We Grodatts are not as concerned with the Whys and Hows of life as you offworlders seem to be."

"And you are not an offworlder?"

"Oh probably we were, then again maybe not. Regardless of where we came from, or where we are headed, we are more interested in the journey than the end of the trip. And I think here lies the difference between my people and others."

"And who are your People?" I asked.

"My people are people who are the same as me. You still have strong suspicions about me for something or other-- Don't you?" Dilbo said" with great amusement.

"Yes I do."

"Soon the Great Gathering will be held, and as the caller you have the right to question all and every life form present."

"All will come?"

"They always have to my best recollections." Dilbo said, and I could feel that this conversation was anything but uncomfortable to him. "You are going to have the chance to hold what your people call a court."

"And what role will I play?" I asked.

"You can be the judge, prosecutor, and jury-- If you want."

"And will you be the accused?" I said, watching for his tell, but he remained impassive.

"As to being the accused--It seems that your contention is that I am guilty of something or other, mainly because I could call the gathering together. It appears that you have just done that very thing yourself. So, by your own logic, you are guilty of whatever you think I'm guilty of. And as a matter of fact all the Grodatts could be suspect, for the talking-devise is always available for any to use that can enter the sanctuary."

"I'm not accusing you of anything Dilbo, and I am hoping that you will be there for me at the Gathering."

"To be sure I'll be there."

"But will you be there for me?" I asked, angrily.

"Of course!" Dilbo said, hugging me suddenly without even being aware that he was doing it. This really left me confused for I could read nothing but good intentions toward me. And body language was always true to itself.

"I don't mistrust you Dilbo. It's just that I am not that clever, and I know that if I don't solve this real soon I won't be able to. I know that I am already operating at a real diminished capacity."

"Never fear good friend, I'll always be here for you, and my capacity has never been more undiminished. Trust me, between us we can unravel who or what is controlling this planet."

"I'm sorry I mistrusted you Dilbo. I know you could never be anything but a friend."

"Come, let's go to the Wild Piggoty inn."

A GREAT GATHERING

For over a week week nothing
happened, and I was beginning to
become convinced that Dilbo had
been playing a trick on me.

"Dilbo are you sure that there is
going to be a meeting?"

"Tink, I am not sure of anything,
as I leave this type of convoluted
logic to others, but I believe
that there is to be a Gathering of
all who heard the calling."

My suspicions and paranoid
thoughts grew. Then, I felt a
murmuring throughout the village
as strangers came in from the
desert. First in ones and twos.
Then, in droves. They came in
airbags, flopping about, just on
the edge of control. A flotilla of
driftwood with sails swept ashore,
and sundry creatures crept,

hobbled and boldly strode in out of the desert.

Soon, a great camp had formed. Circular in shape, yet with no particular definition, nor sign of order. Without any conscious volition, the circular encampment was geometrically perfect. It was as if the encampment had grown up around the toadstool known as Mhyn.

"Who we Watermen be thankin fer da Gatherin?" MaQuig asked Dilbo.

"The Great Gathering has been called by my good friend, Marples Tinkerman. You do remember him don't you?" Dilbo replied.

"Course I be rememberin. Think I be'n Airhead?"

"What dat supposed ta mean? You be lookin fer trouble with us airfolk? We don't go round callin yer waterheads. Many as do, but not ussen airfolk do dat." Agustus

Fung stated, looking down at the motley group of Watermen.

"Din't suspect yer did, yer bein a gennlman n all. Us high officers a water'n wind gots ta be standin tall together. That yer pinion brother Fung?" MaQuig said, huffing all the while, with his face bloated red, and his large, veined eyes all but jumping off his wattled face. He did look around for a small outcropping to stand on, so he was not addressing Fung's crotch.

"We all be standing together. For the Mhyn is starting to thrum, and when it turns white, we will be locked into the Gathering until it returns to green," Dilbo said.

"Just like a traffic light of old," I said, grinning.

"Don't know what you be sayin, but, don spect it be nice ter us dat blongs dis place. What say dat?" MaQuig huffed.

The Windwalkers Of Xambic

"Just meant I didn't expect it was time to start," I replied, not wanting any alienation if I expected to reach any type of conclusion.

MaQuig huffed and puffed, to the amusement of all present.

The humming became stronger and soon it was difficult to hear anyone more than five feet away. For some reason unknown to me, I found myself walking out into the desert, as did everyone. Again, a circle was formed, leaving the center open. Without being told where to sit, everyone had found a place of choice, and not always with their own grouping. I found myself in the eye of the circle.

The humming encircled us like a living force, yet, within the circle it was silent. From the very center I could hear clearly the farthest voice, partly because the sand gradually sloped down to the center, creating a natural amphitheater and moreover because of the power of the Mhyn.

Winnie Minniplant came forward and hugged me. "Not knowing the ways of our one branch. I will help you through your quest. Or do you wish help from another?"

"No. you are fine. Actually, I was hoping for your help. I would like to tell everyone why I have called this Gathering. I should first introduce myself to all of you that do not know me. And for those of you that do, I will explain why I am here."

"Yer here cus yer lost yer ship," scoffed MaQuig.

"True. I did splash down. And not with any design, I might add. Then again, I don't suppose any other than the Singers have any choice about coming and going. That is not unless you have anything to tell us Admiral." I said, looking to Scram.

"Course I gots lots ta say..." MaQuig started to say.

Scram looked to Nhioby.

"For the moment I was addressing Scram or is it Lord Scram, or has Scram got anything to do with your name?" I said looking to the only pilot who was known to have set his ship's coordinates for Xambic.

Scram stood up and opened his mouth to reply but just stood there with a stunned look on his face.

Winnie looked at Scram with more than a little amusement in her violet eyes. "Scram, or whatever your name really is... while I am addressing you, I am also telling all present that it is not possible to lie at a Gathering for the harder you resist the truth, the more painful it will become, and if the caller of the Gathering insists on an answer... Loss of mind... Even death can be the outcome. So, I strongly advise all present to not even consider playing with the truth... Even you my fine queen of Nhark, for I see your amusement," Winnie said.

Nhioby stood tall and regal, her presence one of dominance over the small Twigg, yet she did not reply. A confused look came over her face as she repeatedly tried to answer the Twigg.

"When you decide on the truth, words will come freely," came the amused voice of Winnie.

Prince Nyzerbad, her consort and the ruler of all the Nyzan Empire helped his lovely, but confused, queen to her seat in the sand. She sat stunned. Never had her powers been so easily pushed aside.

"I am glad that you decided to challenge the Mhyn mighty queen, for most here know of your unkept secret of just being a brain damaged trader. Most here know of your awesome powers. With possibly the exception of the Singers."

"Nhioby ...Nhioby ...Nhio--" came the voices of many of the Singer entourage.

"I see that all know of you-- Now!" Winnie said quietly.

"I will answer as I am believing that what is here called a Gathering-- is in my Galaxy-- Known as The Moment." Scram replied.

"Then I am right in supposing that you are possibly more than an addle-headed airbagger?" came my question, but it came from the mouth of Winnie.

I sat on a small flat stone... And smiled inwardly.

"I amuse Marples Tinkerman." came a friendly voice from inside my head. A stern but friendly voice.

"Yes, but I trust you." I answered in the circle of truth.

"Marples would you permit me to be your voice?" Winnie spoke aloud for all to hear.

"I would be honored," I replied, not even bothering to consider how she would know what questions I wanted asked.

Somehow I knew I could trust this small person.

As we were about to resume the interrogation of Scram, the very Comalomg that had followed me ever since my landing came down through the gathering. I noticed that the other Comalongs formed a perimeter of woolly bodies around the perimeter. The Comalong was carrying a small golden suitcase. It calmly entered the circle, placed the golden box at my feet, snorted at Winnie and left. Why? I asked myself.

During the commotion Scram had left the Gathering.

The Windwalkers Of Xambic

The golden box was higher than the smooth black rock, so I sat on it without thinking about it.

Winnie questioned each and every Airfolk thoroughly, then she questioned the Digabouts to the last person. She then started on the Waterpeople.

"Wait... Wait..." I heard my voice say, and from my own lips. "I wish to speak." I blurted.

"But you are speaking. You are speaking through me. Is that not what you wanted and asked for?" came Winnie's calm voice, aloud for all to hear.

"Yes I agreed to let you speak for me."

"And why do you now want to put yourself through this ordeal? You know that I am only trying to stop the pain for you that comes from being a caller of The Gathering," Winnie said, with genuine interest for my well being in her voice and

377

in her eyes. Those great, lovely
violet eye. Those same lovely eyes
that had stared down the power of
Nhioby. lovely eyes...

"Is this my Gathering? Am I not
the caller?" I demanded standing
on the suitcase, as if putting it
between myself and this very
strange planet. "Is this my
Gathering?" I demanded of Winnie.
feeling sick and on the edge of
vertigo.

Slowly the vertigo settled down
and from on top of the golden box
I looked to the crowd. "Is this my
calling?" I asked, confused,
looking from face to face.

Every voice rose to greet my plea.

"Let the caller speak hisself"
MaQuig spluttered. "His own
Calling... Should be his..."

One after the other the crowd rose
to their feet and in a single
voice came a roar, "Let the caller
speak."

"I only have tried to absorb the pain of being the Asker," came a soft faraway voice that held no danger... But!

"Am I to speak? Or..."

Again the roar from the crowd. Over and over they roared, "Let the caller speak."

Quickly, I asked my first question. "Who are you?"

"Who am I?" came a voice gentle and familiar, yet I could detect it being guarded.

"Yes. Who are you?" I demanded of Winnie Minniplant.

"I am Winnie Minniplant. Everyone here knows this."

"You are a Twigg and nothing more?" I asked.

Winnie struggled to speak.

"Are you a Twigg?" I asked, deciding on one question at a

time. More than one question could give honesty a loophole.

"I am of Twigg ancestry,"Winnie said.

"Of Twigg ancestry?" Now isn't this an ambiguous answer for a person who just minutes ago professed to be my friend?"

"I am your friend," Winnie said strongly.

"Yes, I believe you are my friend, however we are here not to find out about the nature of friendships. We are here to try and find out the strangeness that makes this planet a prison."

"Oh no! Never a prison... "Winnie gasped.

"Back to my first question. Are you the mother of Dilbo or not? A simple yes or no is fine."

""No." Winnie said simply.

"But you are related?"

"Yes I am."

"Can you tell us of this Gathering how you are related, being truthful and straightforward in all instances?"

Dilbo strode forward. "You have no call to speak..."

"Sit down my friend. You will be called and have your turn at finally telling the truth." I said, with mounting strength. "Once more I ask you for the truth, Winnie.'

"Dilbo is not my son... Dilbo is my father."

"Your father?" I replied, not expecting this.

"Yes. Dilbo is my father. Many years ago he married my mother, and she died at my birth, and I am told a terrible death, so the experiment has never been repeated." Winnie said, looking to Dilbo for support.

"Then your mother was a Twigg?" I asked Winnie.

"Is all this really necessary?" Dilbo challenged angrily.

"No I suppose not," I said, removing the coat that my good friend Dilbo had given me for my protection.

"I don't think I'll be needing this any more," I said wrapping the great coat around Winnie, and was not surprised to see that it fit her even more comfortably than it had me.

"Are you not going to demand any more answers from the little one?" came a great booming from one of the giant Windwalkers who sat on the outer perimeter.

I knew the identities of the Windwalkers present. And I knew that one Windwalker was not present. Why? I asked myself. For was not the Great Gathering a call to all?

"No, I can get all the answers I need from Dilbo. You may go, or stay, but the choice is yours Winnie."

Winnie walked slowly to the Twigg that I knew as Tata Windsoother... He who rode in the pocket of Bigbow.

"Before I ask any more questions. I think it is the right time to tell all present who I am and why I am here," I said, getting back up on the gold box.

Somehow, I knew that it was the right thing to do, for the comalong had brought it to me, and never had I any doubt as to the sincerity and honesty of the comalongs. I knew they had absolutely no deceit. And often I wished my intentions were as straightforward as these creatures.

Safely off the planet and on the golden box, I addressed the Gathering: "If I am to ask truth of any here, then I believe it only fair that I return that honesty. So, before I challenge the integrity of any present, I think it only fair to have my own integrity and reasons open for all to see."

To my great surprise I was given absolute approval by all present. Even the Singers hissed their approval. However, they were the first to challenge. "Could you tell us your name and state your credentials?" the Noble Khriii twittered in her clear bell-like voice.

I replied without conscious volition. "I am known properly as Captain Marples Tinkerman."

"And you have no other names?" the Khriii twittered.

"The Grodatts have named me Big Tink Noleaf." I grinned.

"I was rather thinking of names that others than us here might know you by," the Bhazz, known as Khriii, twittered.

"No, I have always been Marples Tinkerman and have been a captain for longer than I can presently remember."

"Yes, and that brings me to my next question. Roughly, give or take a century or two, how old are you?"

"As near as I can remember I am about four thousand."

"Four thousand what?"

"Four thousand years as measured by Sol three." I answered.

"Is that an average age for those of Sol three?"

I could see where the clever Bhazz was headed, but could not even consider other than the truth. "No, the lifespan of a native of Sol three is about three hundred Sol years.

"Yet you state you are over four thousand. What do you expect us here make of this incredible fact?"

"First-- you know I am telling the truth. And secondly, the answer is simple-- far in the past I was stranded at a lake, with my ship damaged beyond repair. Radiation from her trimery drive unit seeped into the lake, and somehow drinking and bathing in the waters extended my life."

"Isn't radiation lethal to your species?"

"Certainly," I replied, tired of the questions.

"Then, how did you survive?"

"I have no idea, but unless this questioning is leading somewhere, we have a problem here to solve"

"My next question will clarify my reasoning. What was the name of that planet you were stranded on?" The Bhazz hissed.

"It was Rha" I answered.

"Rha! The birthplace of the RhaEve?"

"Was it not about four thousands of your years ago that the RhaEve made her appearance on Rha?"

"Are you asking me if I am a spy for the RhaEve?"

"I am saying that you are and have always been an agent for the great One."

"That being the case-- Why would I be calling this Great Gathering? Believe me, I am not stuck here of my own accord."

"Obviously not, for untruths are not utterable at this place, not even by the Twiggs!" Chittered the Bhazz angrily.

"Do you have any more questions of me?" I asked.

"No. We of the Kha believe you are an officer of the Federation and nothing more." the Bhazz twittered with what I could detect to be humor.

"I be goten a question," MaQuig said, with a flourish of his smelly old admiral's hat.

"Ask away good friend," I said, smiling at his crew.

"All we Watermen be wantin ta know is iffen we hafta leave Xambic--- be the problem solved? And I wanta know-- am I still ta be accepted bein an Admural n all..."

"Assuredly. My Federation will accept your rank. We of the Federation are not into changing or interfering with foreign powers-- we merely observe and report."

"Nothin else?" MaQuig asked suspiciously.

"No, not unless a power such as the one we are seeking, tries to impose their ways on a less poweriul people. We of the Federation don't believe that might is right. We strive to let all divergent factors of the Federation solve their own internal problems... As long they can do it without taking away the rights of their defenseless neighbors."

"Dat mean a big regular-type navy won't come an push us Watermen around?" MaQuig asked.

"That's exactly our goals."

"N'my rank a Admural be not changed?"

"Not for a second." I said, smiling.

"Den we Watermen be for jinnin da Federation. We done a democrat-type vote, an most agree. Ceptin maybe Meryl. Meryl thinks that he should be n Admural too. What you say bout dat?"

"I think you seem to be able to solve your own problems and we of the Federation would not dare intrude in your navy."

"Dats it! We all fer jinnin. Right me fellow officers?" And to a man the ragged Watermen cheered their leader. This gave me one group that needed no questions about their motives.

The Airfolk led by Augustus Fung quickly proved to be no more in control of anything than the Waterfolk had before them. Only Leklunc moved out of their camp to sit at the feet of his queen, Nhioby. And the allusive Scram had long since deserted their camp.

"I have no reason to question the Queen of Nhark, nor do I have reason to question her consort. Prince Nyzerbad""

And Why not?" a Bha-at challenged.

"Any who have recently arrived are not suspect." I replied

"And why not?" the Bha-at asked, but I knew that he was just making his presence known.

The Windwalkers Of Xambic

"You know as well as I do that this is a situation that has been going on for who knows how long. Do any here know how long Xambic has been pulling starships down?"

Not a reply.

"No matter, for I didn't expect an admission."

"But you have an idea?" Nhioby said, stretching and smiling.

"Yes I do." I replied, also smiling.

"And you have for some time," came a hiss from Nyzerbad.

"No, I am just starting to regain access to my brain, and even now the reason is only vague."

"Yet you expect to clear it up?" came an amused voice from the outer circle.

"Ahhaa! You have returned..." I said, not bothering to turn and see the face of the new arrival.

"You are so sure of your theory?" came the amused voice.

"Oh I know the Whofores of this dilemma. It's the Whatfores that I am not sure of." I replied, turning to face Scram. "Possibly you can shed some light on this problem?" I asked.

"Possibly," Scram said walking down through the crowd. "However, I thought it only fair to let you question me along with all the other good folk of Xambic," Scram said with laughter in his eyes-- laughter that had created very deep laugh-wrinkles around his old eyes.

I had never been this close to Scram before, and had just assumed him to be a young man. Not only was Scram not a young man. Scram was not a man, at least not a man I would know for a man...

"You are amused at my perplexity?" I challenged, looking for a reaction. The crinkling around the

eyes deepened, and I knew this
being bore me no malice.

"You are amused by my struggle?" I
challenged.

"Not as amused as those you seek
to find." Scram replied. "That is
if you are not about to accuse me
of this mischief."

"Scram-- Or whoever you are, you
have alluded to there being
mischief, and those that I am
looking for as being amused. Do
you know the identity of the
culprits?" I asked, knowing that
any present must answer.

Even Nhioby had been forced to
respond to the calling of this
Great Gathering.

"Yes I do." Again the crinkle
around the eyes.

"Then please tell us who has
trapped us and why they have
committed this act against us."

"Oh I doubt they would agree that it is a criminal act. As a matter of fact I agree with them that their act is only one of... Well that is for you to find out. Isn't that the reason for this Gathering?" Scram said, smiling with his mouth and it was a mouth without teeth.

"You have not answered my question."

"Nor do I plan to. I think at this stage in the game it would be unfair to deprive them of the last act."

"The last act?" came from more than one voice in the crowd.

"Will you answer my question?" I continued.

"Actually, I think I will just let you dither around for a little longer," came the highly amused reply.

"You are able to ignore the power of this gathering?"

The Windwalkers Of Xambic

"I ignore all powers wherever I
travel, for it is not my right,
nor my mission to affect changes."

"Does that mean you yourself have
great Powers?" I quickly asked.
hoping to catch Scram off balance.

This brought a great guffawing
from the Windwalkers.

"Actually, I myself have no powers
whatsoever, at least none that you
would consider to be powers."
Scram said.

Again the guffaw from the Giant
Windwalkers.

"Then you are not part of the
conspiracy to bring shipping
down?" I asked already knowing the
answer. And it was an answer that
was making more sense all the
time.

"This problem is not created by
yourself, nor those you
represent?" I continued.

"You know otherwise, come ask me what you are really dying to ask of me." came the soft voice. A voice full of amusement.

"Who are you?" I asked abruptly.

"I am a traveler in space, not unlike yourself Marples Tinkerman."

"Would you call yourself a probe commander?" I asked.

"Actually I could, but no I am not called a deep space probe, commander. As a matter of being correct-- I am not a commander of anything."

This caused the giants to gleefully clap their massive hands with uncontrolled amusement.

"It seems the culprits are in the open." I said addressing the giants directly. "And it may even be obvious why they have committed this act of nuisance."

The Windwalkers Of Xambic

"Be not hasty to judge until the final curtain has been drawn..."

"Until the curtain has been drawn on the last act of this Strange Play?" I cut in.

"Yes, you could say that, but, only could you say it with an absence of malice, for that is how it has been done."

"Malice or not, we are all prisoners on this waterball," I argued just a little peeved. "Whether there has been evil intent, or whether this has been merely a means of amusement, the fact is-- free spacers are held on this planet."

"They never hurted anyone." Bigbow boomed from the back row. "Can any claim hurt from them?"

"We certainly can," interrupted a Bha-at.

"You may think you were damaged, but we only damaged your camp."

Tata Windsoother said with a small voice.

"What of our damaged warriors?" challenged the Khrii.

"Merely an illusion my noble friend."

"What of our dead?" the Bha-at demanded.

"Illusion!" came the small reply from the giant.

"What of our camp? Was that too an illusion?" demanded Tinkle. coming to the Khrii's aid, for the Noble Khriii was showing the pain that came from overusing her seldom used voice.

The Bha-at sat down.

"We of The Tree have never harmed any lifeform," rumbled Windstriker. "Hafta admit Stormrider and I did wreck your camp."

"But you do admit to tampering with free shipping?" I demanded.

398

"We have helped visitors land from time to time." Tata answered.

"And you have helped them to stay forever," I accused.

"Free to go... When they wanted..." came a small petulant reply. from the mighty Stormrider.

"I have a little problem with believing this to be true." I said angrily, "I am a prisoner here, and so are many others. Do you expect me to believe we are able to leave whenever we want?"

"It is the way. Tata Windsoother said softly.

"But what of those who are of second and third generations? Do you expect me to believe they have a choice?" I demanded. They were born here, and want no other life," Tata said.

"What of their parents?" I asked.

"Those that wanted to stay, stayed and the others left."

"How do you justify taking away time?" I asked.

"Time?" Tata asked, then went into a huddle with the other giants. "We aren't sure of what you mean." Tata said.

"We of the Federation are limited in our life expectancy, and if you detain us for years on this planet, those are years of our life that we can never reclaim." I said.

Again they went into a huddle.

"You will see when you leave that you have not lost more than a few clicks of what you would call elapsed time."

"You can do that?" I said, stunned by the enormity of it.

"You will see."

"Why then have we not already been aware of your activities?"

"We have clouded the minds of those sent on." came a very somber reply from Tata Windsoother.

"I understand then that we are all merely players in a play that has been staged for your convenience." I said angrily.

"That is an unkind interpretation. Could we travel, we would visit your cultures and see firsthand the life forces that you enjoy and take for granted." came a sad reply, and it came not from one of the giants...

"Dilbo! What are you saying?" I sputtered.

"I'm saying that we Xambics are never to travel. For we of The Tree must stay close to our tree of life... Or..."

"You are related to these giants?" I asked, confused.

"When you realized that Winnie was my daughter, and not my mother; I thought you had figured it out.

401

Winnie is older than anyone of the inhabitants on Xambic."

"And if you are her fathe--" I said, realizing for the first time how very old Dilbo must be.

"Then you five are the real inhabitants of Xambic?" I asked.

"And your next question is why am I so small and my fellow Xambians are giants?" came Dilbo's amused question.

"It would be the next," I admitted.

As I spoke, Stormrider and Windstriker disappeared, and in their place stood two-- tall, almost identical, elf-like creatures, their skin a pale green. Each elf was obviously male.

"Where are your women?" I asked.

Dilbo had now changed from the familiar shape of a Grodatt, and in his place was another tall elf.

The Windwalkers Of Xambic

"Then you are the missing Giant? You are the KAhoona?"

"Sometimes." came the familiar voice, from the new Dilbo.

"As to our missing women, and in fact our race..."

"Is this painful for you, Dilbo?" I asked.

"No, but it is a long story, and one never told," Dilbo said. "You can call me Dilbo if you like, that is if you will let me call you Tink." my friend said with deep feeling.

"I would like that," I replied, touched by his honesty.

So, the KAhoona of all the Windwalkers told his tale of entrapment. The KAhoona had been created by a creature that lived deep in a well of life-death, and he had been groomed to nurse the Great Tree of Life, that was the beginning to all beings that lived and died, and walked the earths of reality.

His tree was a weak tree that refused to flourish, and stayed barely alive in the Cave of Mhyn Mountain. And while the KAhoona nursed the tree mightily, it would produce no life. The KAhoona pleaded to the Old One in the well for help. The Old One sent up another Keeper for The Tree, this was Tata. And for thousands of years they struggled mightily with The Tree, but the Tree never yielded life ... The KAhoona and Tata pleaded again for help from the Old One. He sent them the Striker to help.

Again, thousands of years went by without life from the tree, and again the KAhoona pleaded, and was sent Rider. And for tens of tens of thousands of earth-years the four Keepers of The Tree of Life, struggled valiantly to make The Tree fulfill its destiny on

The Windwalkers Of Xambic

Xambic. But, it was not to be, and suddenly, the well closed over and the four Keepers were left without guidance or help.

Boredom, confusion, anger at being left without guidance was the fate of the foursome, until the first space traveler landed. Older than old and without purpose of their own, the four Keepers found entertainment in the petty problems of the crashed spacers.

"Then you four are the Twiggs? -- and the Windwalkers?" I asked my friend Dilbo.

"Tis all true!" Tata Windsoother said, sadly.

"Then originally you were not known as the KAhoona, he who is the Lord of the Wind, and in some cases Stormkeeper?" I asked.

Dilbo replied with a grin. "No-- I was originally named: The Keeper of the Tree, and then when the Soother was created, we come to call each other as just Soother and Keeper."

"And the Windstriker was Str-" I started to say.

"Yes I was named Striker." Windstriker said quietly.

"And I was Rider," put in the former Stormrider.

"But with the arrival of larger more aggressive offworlders, you needed some protection, so you assumed these identities?"

"Yes, we have no aggressive war-like characteristics built into us, for we are merely keepers of a tree-- a tree that will not grow, and that is our destiny. As giants who rode the skies we kept offworlders at bay with our size and false ferocity," Dilbo said.

"Then who is Bigbow? And why is he still a giant?" Nhioby purred at Dilbo, but without malice.

"Bigbow is really a giant. He was not guided in by us, and really crashed. The crash ruined his ship. Fortunately we were able to nurse him back to health, but his mental faculties have never returned to him." Dilbo, the KAhoona told Nhioby.

"You just said his ship really crashed," Nhioby purred.

"That's true." Dilbo replied.

"Am I to infer then that our ships have not really crashed?" Nhioby continued excitedly.

"Only the ones that we helped down are intact." Dilbo replied. "We are guilty of being bored, and of interrupting a few journeys for a matter of what you would term as clicks, but nothing more." Dilbo said, turning red.

"Clicks-- You say that you have only interrupted us for clicks?" I asked, not believing my ears. "Something is remiss here my good

407

friend, for I have been here for years."

"So it would appear-- for now! But, when the final curtain falls on this little play, then you may draw your own conclusions... Not yet."

"Then we are merely players in a play?" I challenged.

"Can we be more?" Dilbo replied, without thinking.

"That is a greater question than I am prepared to tackle, at least without a little kakleberry to ease the way." I replied.

"About our ships," Nhioby said, unamused.

"You, my good lady do not have ships, you arrived on a dragon class Battle-wagon... And it is safe." Tata said, with great amusement and reprimand in his clear voice.

"Then I am free to leave?" Nhioby asked.

"Whenever you wish to," said the former Stormrider.

The KAhoona. He who can talk to all things living, did just that. He sat and hummed a head-ache hum that brought forth thousands of the elusive Sandshrieks. A great quiet followed, and the Sandshrieks were gone as quickly as they had arrived.

"You communicate with-- them?" Nhioby asked with interest.

"My lord, the KAhoona speaks with all things living, the Old One in the Well might better have named him Speaker instead of Keeper," the former Windstriker said, grinning at Dilbo.

Out of the sand rose a dark, sinister ship. And it was a Battlewagon of Nhark design.

"You are free to leave..." Dilbo said quietly.

"You will be sorry about your little game. When the combined might of Nyzan and Nhark are finished with this planet-- it will be less than a waterball!" And they left for their ship.

The four Keepers of The Tree smiled.

"Am I to gather they will remember nothing?" I asked Dilbo.

"Those that come of their own accord by way of natural disaster, we do nothing about, but those we detain from time to time are eventually sent about their way." Dilbo said.

"And you feel no guilt?" I demanded.

"Do you feel guilt for borrowing a book that has important information you require?" Dilbo replied.

"But I..."

"You don't harm the book. And it's only purpose is to supply you with entertainment, or information-- right?" Dilbo said, as if to a very small child. "Well we too have needs, and so we borrow a few clicks from passers-by, for our simple needs."

"I don't understand how you equate us with books, and I have no idea how you claim to only take clicks from our lives." I said, angry with their cavalier attitude about interrupting our lives.

"Yes, we see that you have no understanding about time. As a matter of fact-- the time we borrow from your busy lives only amounts to what in your understanding would be seconds. My good friend Tata has corrected me about us taking clicks, and is now insisting that we do not even take clicks as you would know them. So there is no damage done... Only information gained."

Even as we spoke the Massive Battlewagon disappeared. It did not rise up majestically on it's repulsion unit, then phomag into deep space, it simply disappeared.

This calling of ships repeated itself until all the kidnapped offworlders had left.

Old Drifter sat upon the sand waiting for me.

"We'll have to realign TC," Dilbo said looking to the golden box I was standing on earlier.

"TC is in that box?"

"Yes, we have been very busy with her since you arrived. It is intelligence from such as her that will eventually free us."

"You are captives?" I asked.

"We are the only captives. And will remain as such until we can coax The Tree of Life to grow... or we are freed from this obligation." Dilbo said, watching a comalong take the box to my spaceprobe.

"Will I remember any of what transpired here?" I asked. "Only for yourself." Dilbo said.

"Then my report for the Feder-"

"It will be honest. It will say that this sector is secure, and that it is a simple class-3 planet that is inhabited by several cultures living in harmony, and living far below the ability to protect themselves from outsiders."

"This will mean an automatic quarantine from all Federated ships until you are able to protect yourselves," I said, smiling.

"True... And look about you: Do these harmless peoples not need a big brother to watch over them?"

"I suppose so..." I started to say.

Deepspace... And I knew my mission was complete.

"TC, let's head for home." I said to my companion.

"Your wish is my command," came the musical laughter of TC.

DEBRIEFING

I sat waiting for the Octumvarite to read my report.

"Captain Tinkerman, your report shows that the mission was routine and that it is your opinion that the Alpheratz system should be quarantined until the natives develop sufficient technology to represent themselves in the Federation. Also, we see that the Singers are representing no threat to the well-being of the natives. Is there anything you want to say off the record, Captain Tinkerman?"

"Only that the Singers have a small internal situation that could eventually develop into a problem... But it is not of a nature to ever endanger the Federation," I replied, knowing that if Dilbo could have seen me

415

trying to report all that I really knew--Dilbo would be laughing at my discomfort.

And somehow I knew he was.

"You are dismissed captain, and we commend you on a job done in record time..."

THE END